THE BIRDS
HAVE ALSO GONE

Yashar Kemal was born in 1923 in the small village, Hemite, which lies in the cotton-growing plains of Chukurova. Later, in Istanbul, he became a reporter on the newspaper *Cumhuriyet* and in 1952 he published a book of short stories, *Yellow Heat*. In 1955 came his first novel *Ince Memed*, published in English under the title *Memed, My Hawk*. This won the Varlik Prize for the best novel of the year. His novels include *Beyond the Mountain* (3 volumes), *The Legend of Ararat*, *The Drumming-Out*, *The Legend of the Thousand Bulls*, *Murder in the Ironsmiths Market* (3 volumes), *To Crush the Serpent*, *The Saga of the Seagull*, *The Sea-Crossed Fisherman*, *Little Nobody* and *The Pomegranate Tree on the Knoll*. Other published works include a volume of *Collected Short Stories*, *Essays and Political Articles*, *God's Soldiers* (Reports on Delinquent Children), and a novel for the young, *The Sultan of the Elephants and the Red-Bearded Lame Ant*.

Yashar Kemal is married and has one son. His wife, Thilda Kemal, translates his books into English.

YASHAR KEMAL

THE BIRDS HAVE ALSO GONE

A novel translated from Turkish by
Thilda Kemal

Minerva

A Minerva Paperback

THE BIRDS HAVE ALSO GONE

First published in Great Britain 1987
by Collins Harvill
This Minerva edition published 1989
by Methuen · Mandarin
Michelin House, 81 Fulham Road, London SW3 6RB

Minerva is an imprint of the Octopus Publishing Group

Copyright © Yashar Kemal 1978
Copyright in the English translation © Thilda Kemal 1987

British Library Cataloguing in Publication Data

Kemal, Yashar, *1922–*
The birds have also gone
Rn: Kemal Sadik Gokçeli   I. Title
II. Kuslar da gitti. *English*
894′.3533[F]   PL248.Y275

ISBN 0 7493 9015 8

The Random House Group Limited supports The Forest Stewardship
Council® (FSC®), the leading international forest-certification organisation.
Our books carrying the FSC label are printed on FSC®-certified paper.
FSC is the only forest-certification scheme supported by the leading
environmental organisations, including Greenpeace. Our
paper procurement policy can be found at
www.randomhouse.co.uk/environment

MIX
Paper | Supporting
responsible forestry
FSC® C018179

Printed and bound in Great Britain by Clays Ltd, St Ives plc

PRONUNCIATION GUIDE

Letter	Approximate pronunciation
a	as in French *avoir*, English *man*
c	j as in *jam*
ç	ch as in *church*
e	as in *bed* or the French *e*
g	as in *goat*
ğ	a soft g that lengthens the preceding vowel and never occurs at the beginning of a word
h	as in *house*
o	like French *eau*
ö	as in German *König*, French eu in *deux*
s	as in *sing*
ş	sh as in *shall*
u	as in *push*
ü	as in German *führer*, French u in *tu*
y	as in *yet*

1
〜〜〜

Tuğrul came walking along the fringe of the wood and stopped by the tents.

Though it was not yet mid-September, three boys from the old quarter of Fatih had already set up a tent near the aged poplar on the eastward side of the green meadow and had even begun to weave clap-nets and place snares. They kept at it from early dawn to nightfall, humming strange old tunes as they worked. One of the boys was short and broad-shouldered. He had large hands and a huge head with hair that stuck out stiff as quills. His three-cornered eyes were marked by casts. The one in his left eye spread right into the dark iris. He hardly ever uttered a word, only opening his mouth to sing. The second boy was tall as a beanpole, with a long neck and bulging eyes that seemed about to pop out of their sockets. This one talked twenty to the dozen, stopping abruptly with his thin neck stretched taut, longer than ever. The third boy was one of those tough city urchins, a real firebrand, never still for a moment. His hands were constantly occupied making and unmaking things while he talked, shouted and teased his companions. Yet his blue-grey eyes were infinitely sad, and though his chin jutted out in a strong curve, there was something sad about it too. A thin yellow moustache, only just sprouting, drooped over his lip and, whenever his hands were free, he tugged at it angrily, as though determined to pluck it off.

Tuğrul settled down on a mound in front of the barbed wire that fenced in the ancient poplar. For the past ten days I had seen him sitting there, hugging his knees to his chin, unmindful of the thistles that covered the mound, sometimes even leaning on the barbed wire. Strangely enough, he never looked at the noisy bustling boys, nor did he lift his head at the roar of the helicopters and airplanes that passed low over the field.

On Sundays that police chief from Kinali Island would always be there, flying one of those toy planes that are operated from the ground. And not only the police chief, but many others too came to this flat field behind Florya beach. They arrived in posh cars, Mercedes, Volvos, Volkswagens, Murats, to fly their toy planes which made more noise than any real airplane as they whirled and dived in the skies above Florya. Crowding around them would be children from the suburbs of Çekmece, Menekşe, Cennetmahallesi, and even from as far away as Yeşilyurt, all watching in awed reverence, silent, quite still, only their eyes moving from the toy plane to the person who controlled it.

Not once did Tuğrul look up, not even when a helicopter whirred low above him, almost licking the crest of the big poplar. It could have crashed right there beside him for all he seemed to care. So many times I walked past him, but he did not see me. Or did it only seem so? Perhaps he saw it all. Perhaps he did not miss a single thing taking place on the plain, saw the glowing radiance cast by the sea over the land, heard the chug-chug-chug of the fishing boats and caught the salty tang and the odour of rotting seaweed and iodine, moist and warm and penetrating.

One fine morning, I found the wide expanse of Florya Plain dotted with bird snares. They had been set up everywhere, along the fringe of the wood, on the little slope that inclined towards the railroad, under the almond and fig trees, beside the clump of poplars and even among the patches of thistles. Children, men, young and old, well-dressed or down-at-heel, lottery hucksters, three-card tricksters, apprentices to repair workshops, or to blacksmiths and tailors, small-time fishermen, one and all had spread their clap-nets, tied their live decoys to a string and placed the cages containing the captured songbirds around them. They knelt on the ground, their eyes fixed on the sky, uttering bird-like whistles that rose to a crescendo whenever a flight of birds showed up in the distance.

The greenfinch is a darkish ash-grey bird, slightly smaller than the sparrow. The goldfinch is yellow. Then there is the chaffinch, the coal titmouse and a host of other tiny bright-coloured birds, yellow-breasted, the most brilliant of yellows, or red, flame-like, or green, all so vivid you can see them even in the dark. And there is the blue one, no bigger than a thumb, flashing like a ball of blue light through the sky, leaving a fulgent blue trail in its wake.

Tuğrul was there as usual, his chin on his knees, his arms hugging his legs.

"Hello, Tuğrul."

He pretended not to hear, but his right shoulder twitched.

"Come now, Tuğrul! I said hello to you. What are

you doing, sitting here, day in, day out?"

His back heaved and his frail scraggy neck shrank even lower between his shoulders. A leaf from the poplar tree fluttered down and rested on his foot.

I sat down beside him and laid a hand on his shoulder.

"What's the matter, Tuğrul?"

Slowly he turned to me, a little embarrassed perhaps, his eyes glowing, as though with tears. He tried to smile, but his thin cracked lips froze. Then he bent his head again.

"Nothing's the matter, Abi,"* he mumbled.

"But there is," I insisted.

"Well, there is, then!" he flared up. "Why should I care?"

"Care about what, Tuğrul?"

"All that!" He gestured angrily towards the tent. "Those fellows there. . ."

"What's wrong with them?"

He glared at me and relapsed into silence.

I gave up and left him to himself.

I was quite annoyed with Tuğrul. Why didn't he speak out like a man and tell me what was going on in that tent? Perhaps he was vexed now that I hadn't insisted a little more, perhaps he would never speak to me again. Well, that was his problem.

But after this, every time I passed that way, I stopped and took a closer look at the tent and its inmates. Nothing unusual was taking place there as far as I could see. The three boys, like everyone else, had fixed a clap-net, positioned a few cages with songbirds around them, and fastened their decoys. Whenever a

* abi: big brother.

flight of birds passed above, they pursed their lips in a loud whistle, and if the birds alighted on the thistles, they swiftly pulled the net down, their hearts bounding, their eyes almost popping out. And in the same instant they shot out, the three of them as one, in a hectic eager sprint to the trapped birds that were fluttering frantically in the meshes of the net.

In the end, curiosity got the better of me. Like Tuğrul, I too sat down to watch, but on the opposite side of the tent, under the old terebinth. Then I noticed Tuğrul giving me a meaningful look.

Each time a flight of birds appeared in the sky, alighted on the thistles and were crammed into the big cages by the boys in a screeching welter of bright colours, Tuğrul's eyes went from the sky to the net, from the boys to the cages. Then he lowered his head to his knees again, until a fresh flight of birds came to rest on the thistles, until again the boys were scampering up to the closed net with cries of triumph.

My evening walk would often take me past the old poplar tree, and one night what should I see but Tuğrul, sitting there in his accustomed place, though it was quite late. A bright light issued from the tent, and the sound of voices too. One of the boys was laughing, a fitful broken sound, more like sobbing than laughter, more like a lament, like the note of some strange bird. I could have sworn it was that beanpole lad who was laughing so. I stopped a little way from Tuğrul and called to him.

He made no answer. Did his back heave, his shoulder tremble? It was too dark to see.

"Tuğrul, Tuğrul," I called again.

Very slowly, he rose and brushed his clothes with

11

both hands. Then he walked off towards the seashore, not even bothering to look at me. His stooped figure, round as a ball in the darkness, disappeared among the shanties.

A fire was burning in front of the tent, and now and again one of the boys, the short tough one, would come out to gather thistles from round about and throw them onto the fire.

2

The boys were always up very early in the morning, but even before they had woken, at the first glimmer of dawn, Tuğrul would be there already. How many times had I seen him rushing along the fringe of the wood towards the poplar tree, as though fearful of missing something, and then, if the boys were still asleep, he would draw a deep breath and slump down in his accustomed place in front of the barbed wire, resting his chin on his knees.

On Florya Plain, the bird hunt was in full swing now. So it is each year when October comes, when the north wind is blasting, ice-cold, keen as a razor's edge, or when the sea is churned into a furious foaming mass by the *lodos* that blows from the south. Then, clouds of tiny birds are tossed hither and thither, tracing zigzags in the air, flurrying down over the thistles, only to rise again in the same instant, veering swiftly over the sea, on to Çekmece Lake and back to the wood, grazing the crests of the trees, a scatter of many-coloured specks in the sky, vanishing from sight and appearing again. But on warm sunny days, they swarm down over the thistles in thousands, twittering madly, and devour with frightening rapacity the seeds of the dried shrubs that, in the summer, had flowered bright yellow, dyeing the whole plain saffron.

Ever since ancient Byzantium, through Ottoman times to this day, these tiny birds, coming no one knows whence and going no one knows where, have sojourned here, on Florya Plain, from October to the end of December. And ever since, the people of Istanbul town have set all kinds of snares to capture them. They capture them, and then sell them, in front of churches if they are Christians, synagogues if they are Jewish, or mosques if they are Moslems. "Fly little bird, free as the air, and meet me at the gates of Paradise." And so, all over Istanbul town, the sky will be swarming with little birds delivered from captivity by those who wish to ensure a place in Paradise cheaply. Children especially, and also the very old. . .

Many years ago, it must have been when I first came to Istanbul, I had seen in Taksim Square a very old gentleman, wearing a fur-collared coat, and a little boy of six or seven. From a barefooted youngster they were buying tiny wild-eyed yellow birds and casting them up into the air. They would take it in turns, first the old gentleman, then the little boy, and at every throw the three of them would cry out in pure joy. And there was that cat huddling in the bushes under the plane trees. . . Every now and again, one of the small birds, unable to take wing, would fall to the ground and flutter off into the bushes. No sooner there than that monster of a cat would pounce on it, tear it apart with claws and teeth, and devour it greedily. Then, licking its chops, the cat would lie in wait, quite still, its eyes on the air, for its next prey.

Nowadays, it is only in the courtyard of Eyup Mosque that children manage to sell a bird or two to be set free. So they prefer to take them to the bird market

14

in Eminönü where the dealers select a few of the finest out of hundreds, in order to sell them at a high price to bird fanciers. And the children go back home, weary, disappointed, toting their cages still filled to the brim, wondering what to do with all these birds.

If the chroniclers of Istanbul city neglect the history of these birds and of the fowlers on Florya Plain, then their work, according to me, will not be worth much. Indeed, it will all have been in vain. The joy of millions of little birds set free in front of churches, synagogues and mosques for hundreds of years, and the joy of so many people too... Is that an adventure of small importance? One day, I know it, some person, imaginative, wise, pure of heart, will come forward and write the fine history, full of hope and gladness, of the birds of Florya Plain, and then Istanbul city will be a more beautiful, a more enchanting place. Is the magic of Istanbul only in its sea and sky, its rivers and monuments? And what of the Florya birds then?

A few days later, I saw that another lad had joined Tuğrul. They were sitting side by side, chin on knees, just like that. And not two days had gone by before six were squatting on the mound in front of the barbed wire fence, hugging their knees, staring vacantly into space. Were they angry, crazy, pensive? Their faces gave nothing away.

The boys from the tent darted busily here and there, calling to the birds, agitating their decoys and bringing down the clap-net over the thistle shrubs. Now and again they cast a glance at the motionless group on the mound, perplexed by their strange attitude. Soon, a second cage was filled. Then a third. And now there were eight cages in the tent, all crammed with terrified little birds, yellow, red, blue, their eyes rolling like gleaming grapeshot, fluttering madly as they knocked against the wire of the cages in a frenzied attempt to escape. The cages were of the ordinary kind, fifty centimetres wide, eighty long and sixty high.

These boys from Fatih. . . Now I come to think of it, who had told me they came from Fatih? I don't know. Perhaps it just seemed so to me. Maybe I said to myself, that's the quarter of the town which suits them best. . . Well, these Fatih boys had begun to look with growing bewilderment at the silent group of six on the mound, with a little bit of fear too. . .

They were in luck this year. The birds had come in great numbers and there were some in those cages that they had never seen before, did not even know their names. They had caught six of one rare kind with pure red plumage that grew paler under the wings and on the breast, and each one was sure to sell for seven liras at least. They had captured a falcon too and put it in a separate cage. Every day, they fed it with half a dozen live goldfinches and chaffinches, and the rapacious bird, its anger sharpened by captivity, would tear the little birds to pieces the instant it had them in its talons, just like that cat.

Yet falcons are quite rare in these parts. Maybe this one had come all the way from the Istranca forests in pursuit of the migrant birds. From high up, it had swooped down over the live decoy of the Fatih boys and, just as it grasped the tiny goldfinch, the net had closed over it. The children had tried to wrest the goldfinch from its talons, but the falcon had lashed out at them with its beak. Their hands were all torn and bloody.

16

It was a motley-feathered falcon. They sold it to Gypsy Halil for thirty-five liras. Then they bagged two brown hawks which Gypsy Halil again bought from them for twenty-five liras each. The gypsy would take these birds to Kavak village and re-sell them to the hunters there at a good profit.

3

~~~

Way up, high over the sea, a bird of prey was circling in the sky. I went up to the tent.

"Look," I said. "That's a falcon."

"We've seen it," the short boy said, the one who had triangular eyes.

"Will it come down, d'you think?"

"It's sure to, in a little while, but..." He sighed.

"But what?"

"The trouble is, Abi, these birds tear the net to rags. What's more, nobody wants them except Gypsy Halil. And he only pays twenty-five or thirty liras for each bird. It's not worth it."

The beanpole lad was dying to speak. "It's killing work to catch them, takes you a whole day. And the way they charge down at the decoys! I got the fright of my life yesterday..."

"Well, try and catch this one," I said.

The boy's long neck stretched up towards the bird. "It'll soon be here," he observed, and his neck remained extended, longer than ever.

The short one made a face. "Not for me, thanks," he said.

"Catch it for me," I insisted.

Their eyes shone. "What'll you give us?"

I thought it over. "A hundred liras," I said.

18

"Hurray!" cried the short boy.

The beanpole lad's neck stretched to breaking point towards the bird. "Come, come, come. . ." he called. He turned to me. "It won't be long," he assured me.

"You can wait in the tent, Abi, if you like," the short boy said. "We'll soon catch that bird and bring it to you."

"All right," I said. I sat down in front of the tent. From inside came the clamour of hundreds of caged birds.

"A hundred liras. . ." the tough boy murmured, the restless one. Quickly he adjusted the string to the net. "A hundred liras," he repeated. He gazed up at the sky. The bird was lower now, floating above the presidential summer residence. I could hear the boy muttering to himself. "A hundred liras, a hundred. . . And another one, that'll make two hundred liras. Good. . . Five, ten, twenty falcons. . . Two thousand liras. . ."

He made a game of it, the tough little urchin, matching his motions to the rhythm of his litany, almost dancing as he checked the net and tugged again and again at the string to lift the decoys up into the air. The bird of prey hovered in the blue of the sky behind the veil of vapour rising from the sea, its wings outspread, quivering slightly, swaying this way and that in the blowing north-easter.

Eagerly, the tough boy ran up to me. He looked taller now. "How many of those birds will you buy if I catch them?" he asked. He pointed at the falcon. "Look, Abi, how it flies! Isn't it beautiful?"

"Indeed it is," I said.

"It'll be yours in no time," he said.

Hurrying back to the clap-net, he tugged at the string

19

and four tiny yellow decoy birds shot up in a desperate attempt to fly, only to be pulled down to the height of one metre by the string tied to the small prongs attached to their feet. The boy drew the string once more and up went the birds again. He kept making the decoys spring into the air, fixing a watchful eye on the bird of prey as it floated calmly in the sky.

After a while, he was back again by my side.

"How many of these birds are you going to buy?" he asked.

"Let's see you catch them first," I said. "If I can't buy them all, we can always sell them."

"Who to?" he inquired sceptically.

"Well, to Skipper Hasan, for one," I said.

"Who's he?"

"He's a sea captain," I said. "A neighbour of ours. A Laz from the Black Sea. He used to own many birds like this one. They say he's a first-rate hunter."

"Lazes are good hunters," the boy stated with an important air. "But what if he doesn't buy them?"

"Then I will. I'll give him one as a present."

"Isn't there anyone else around here?"

"There's Ali Bey, the police officer, the one who takes people's fingerprints."

"Fingerprints! You don't say!"

"Yes, indeed," I assured him. "He's a neighbour too. And before he became a police officer, when he was still living in Rize, he had five of these birds and he went hunting for quails with them, day and night, bagging whole baskets of quails. You know those wide Black Sea baskets?"

"Wow!"

"And as for Skipper Hasan. . ." I pointed to the sky.

"He gave me the names of seven species of those birds, those hawks... And Ali Bey..."

"That's not a hawk, it's a falcon," the tough boy corrected me. His name was Semih. The boy with the three-cornered eyes was called Hayri, and the other one, the beanpole lad, was Süleyman. But no one ever called him by his name. They all addressed him as Longy.

He now came and crouched in front of me. "Abi," he said, pointing to Tuğrul and his friends, "who are those?"

"That's Tuğrul," I said. "He's from our neighbourhood, the son of the head night watchman at Menekşe. The other one's Hüseyin. And that one with the pointed nose is Erol, a fisher boy. I don't know the other three."

"So," Süleyman murmured, "he's a watchman's son, this Tuğrul..."

"What of it?" I asked.

"Nothing, only that he's here at the crack of dawn every day that God sends..."

"I know..."

Süleyman went on talking about Tuğrul, his eyes, the way he looked at you... A queer one he was, a little crazy, wasn't he?

"True enough," I said.

"Yes, Abi, true, but what do they want with us, those fellows? We're only here to make a little cash."

"Well?"

"But that Tuğrul, he's just taking it easy. Of course he is, seeing his father's a watchman, no less, and at Florya too..."

"Not Florya, Menekşe..."

"But Florya and Menekşe are one, aren't they?" He was almost pleading.

"You could say so, yes."

This seemed to please him. "It was clear," he went on, "that his father was someone important. Look, Abi, just look at those fellows! Are they maniacs, or what? To come here day after day before dawn and sit like that, side by side, without speaking, not a word, just staring across at us all the time. And their eyes! Agate eyes. . ."

"So they are!"

"Well, agate eyes bring bad luck. Why, but for those boys sitting there, that bird would have been in our net long ago. A hungry falcon, and all these decoy birds right under it. . . Would it ever remain swinging up there this long? Yesterday, those falcons were charging at the decoys like hungry wolves. Word of honour, Abi! I had the devil of a time chasing them away. And look how it is today, just when we want to catch one! How I swore and cursed it! Maybe it got offended. Maybe it understood. Can birds understand what we say?"

"Why not?" I said.

"Maybe they do," he said with a doubtful look at the bird, then at Tuğrul.

"All the creatures of this world understand each other," I said.

"Agate eyes, he's got," Süleyman repeated, staring at Tuğrul. "Blue-streaked. . ."

A helicopter had taken off from Yeşilköy and was coming our way from over the sea, flying very low as though it would hit the tall plane tree in front of the Municipal Beach.

"Now this!" Süleyman exclaimed. "Birds don't like

22

those thingummies one bit!"

"It's those eyes," I said. "Agate. . ."

Süleyman laughed, though he cast an even more suspicious look at the boys. All six of them were sitting there in the same posture, legs hugged to their chests, chins resting on their knees, not moving, not looking at anything in particular, just waiting. . .

With a great racket, scattering seagulls all about it, the helicopter barely cleared the plane tree and passed on over the presidential summer residence. All of us, Tuğrul and his friends too, looked up to see if the bird of prey was still there. And so it was. As though nothing had happened, as though stuck to the blue of the sky, its wings outstretched, quivering, it was flying below a very white cloud. How glad we were, all of us, even Tuğrul and his friends. I guessed it from their faces.

The boy Hayri was getting angry now. Furiously, he tugged at the string, hurling the decoys up into the air, and brought them down with a bang. At this rate, the unfortunate birds would not hold out till evening, they'd be dead by midday.

This time, it was Semih who came up to me.

"Something's the matter," he said. "Honest to God, something queer. . ." His face was tense with anxiety. "It's a jinx, that's what it is. Only yesterday those birds were pouncing onto our decoys like wild beasts. . . And now. . . You see for yourself. At the mention of that hundred liras. . . There!" He cast a wary glance in the direction of the six boys. "Ah, we've been jinxed all right," he sighed. "But it'll come. . ." He glared at Tuğrul. "Do what you like, it'll come to us anyway. And how!" He took a turn at tugging the decoys and

23

shouted: "It'll come, yes it will!" His eyes were on the bird, willing it to descend.

"Sure, it'll come," I said.

Just then, from below Basinköy, down by the railway tracks, a large flight of little birds soared into view and in a moment the three boys were all in a bustle, seething with excitement, Süleyman on his knees emitting bird-like sounds to lure the flock, Semih making the decoys fly, and Hayri ready with the rope to the clap-net. All three necks were craned in eager expectation, three pairs of eyes never left the flock of birds that was drawing nearer, surging, sinking, veering hither and thither in the sky. Now they were right above Tuğrul's group, pausing above the old poplar tree, rising, falling... Three of them came to perch on the snare's thornbush and with one voice the decoys started trilling ever more shrilly. The main flock swept off towards the wood. In no time, it was back and five more little birds settled on the thistles, while the rest drifted on above Menekşe. Still Hayri waited. He made no move to pull the rope. And soon the main flock sheered back from over Menekşe, swarming high and low, and alighted in a body on the thornbush. In the same instant, Hayri tugged at the rope and the clap-net closed down over them. Strident twitters broke out, like a clamour, as the trapped birds floundered madly in the net. The three boys at once rushed up and began taking the birds from the net and shutting them up in the cages. Tuğrul and his friends had bounded to their feet the moment the birds were captured and they stood staring, dumbfounded, their eyes wide with what was perhaps anger.

"They're quite full now," Semih said as he walked

up to me. "All the cages... Some days we catch as many as five hundred. When they come like that, you know, you can't not catch them."

"Of course not," I said. "Since you've set up your snares anyway..."

"No, of course not," he echoed. But he seemed crest-fallen all of a sudden.

"You can sell them for 'fly and be free' in Taksim or Sirkeci or Eyup, as always."

"They won't buy them. Nobody buys birds for 'fly and be free' any more. Yesterday, I ranged the whole town. Not a living soul was there who wanted to free a bird, to set it soaring up into the Istanbul skies... People have changed. There's no faith, no religion left in anyone, no conscience, no belief in Allah and the holy book..."

Semih had worked himself into such a passion that the veins in his neck swelled. It was as though he had the faithless, godless population of Istanbul there before him and was taking issue with them. With clenched fists he hit at the air, talking, shouting, beside himself.

"Look, Abi, just look at my feet! See how swollen they are? You wouldn't believe it, all day long, yesterday, there isn't a place in Istanbul I didn't go to, and not one, not a single of Allah's creatures came and said, it's for my afterlife, for my place in Paradise, not one would give two and a half liras to set a little bird free! Istanbul town's nothing but a nest of infidels now, Abi..Look at these birds, Abi. In the old days... Why, only five years ago, my big brother would sell a thousand in a single day, all for 'fly and be free', and he'd make one thousand five hundred liras each day at the coming of the birds. And look at me, Abi, look at my feet. . ."

He grabbed the cage full of screeching birds and swung it in front of me.

"For God's sake, Abi, look! Aren't they beautiful? Wouldn't any man with a spark of human feeling, any good Moslem, any God-fearing person, buy one of these birds to set it free, and not only one but five, ten, forty? What crime have they committed, these tiny little things, to remain cooped up like this in cages, one on top of the other? Won't Allah punish those who see them like this and do nothing to free them? Just look at the poor things, dying to get out, look, look, Abi, wouldn't anyone's heart melt at the state they're in? Every day five or six of them die in this cage, Abi. They die! We didn't catch the poor things to torment them. We thought they'd be set free at once."

His voice was tearful, his face drawn with pain. At a touch, he would be sobbing outright.

"You could take them to the bird market in Eminönü. And what about the Flower Market up in. . ."

"But we did!" Hayri broke in. "Those scoundrels, those dirty thieving bird sellers offered us ten kurush only for each bird! Now, who ever sees a ten-kurush coin these days? Do you, Abi? Does anyone call ten kurush money any more?"

"What scoundrels!" I was beginning to feel as angry as Hayri.

The long boy joined us.

"Me, I went to Eminönü three days ago with two cages full of birds and I barely escaped being killed by a horrible man with a beard. He was in such a rage, snarling, brandishing a stick, too... Like a wild bull, honest to God, he chased me twice round the park, me running for my life, him with that stick, a stick as big as this... It was touch and go. If I hadn't dropped the cages there, in the middle of the park, I would've been done for. He was after me to the death, his beard quivering, his lips twitching. To the death! But I'll get even with him, I will... When he saw that I'd left my cages, the bearded man rushed to them, still snarling, he crouched down, his stick beside him. And me, trembling in all my limbs, I stopped on the steps of Valide Mosque and watched him. And what do you know, he lifted up his hands and for maybe half an hour he recited prayers! Then he opened the cages and let the birds out, and for every bird that flew off he said a prayer, and this went on till noon. Yes indeed, I know, because they were calling the *ezan* for the noonday prayer just as he held the very last bird. For a long, long time he stroked it and prayed and prayed and then he let it go. I was furious, you can imagine. Still, I dared not move. Mad I was, dying to do something, but I was tied hand and foot. And that's not all! The next thing I knew, the bearded man was stamping on my cages, smashing them! By the time he stopped, they were flat as a board. Was I mad! Mad... When I think of what I did with that kilim... My mother's kilim... Why, she had me slung up to the ceiling by the feet and left me hanging upside down like that for a whole day! Such a rug it was, Abi, with the finest embroidery you ever saw. It hung on the wall, and I could sit and watch it for ever, especially when the sun touched it and the colours came alive and flittered here and there... When I think of that kilim..."

"What's all this about a kilim, Longy?"

"Well, Abi, it's like this. . ." Süleyman stopped and swallowed several times.

"He's ashamed now," Hayri observed.

"What about?"

Hayri gave Süleyman a pregnant look. Süleyman was trembling and his face was quite pale.

"If only it hadn't happened," Semih sighed. "If only Longy hadn't done that."

"Done what, for heaven's sake?"

"It wasn't right," Hayri declared. "We should never have let him do it."

All at once Süleyman seemed to come to life. "I sold it," he hissed with a defiant toss of his head.

"Yes, he sold it," Semih mourned. Semih the tough one! There was nothing tough about him now. He looked wretched. "We sold it," he repeated, his voice breaking. "It belonged to his mother, who got it from her own mother when she became a bride. A precious keepsake, it was. Beautiful. . ."

Süleyman cast him a look charged with resentment. "Well, it was you put me up to it," he burst out. "You with your made-up moustache!"

Semih's face changed. "Look here, Longy, don't provoke me," he growled. There was a dangerous gleam in his eyes.

"You can get as provoked as you like," Süleyman retorted, though his tone was less aggressive now. "You can kill me for all the good it'll do us after this."

"It's too late," Hayri said. "The poor woman took to her bed with grief. Who knows, maybe she's dead even. . ."

"I'll get it back," Semih vowed. "There's nothing I

28

wouldn't do for Aunt Zare. Even if I have to die, I'll get it back for her from that man."

He looked at me as though for assistance. "I can get it back, Abi, I'm certain. Can't I?"

"You could try, at any rate," I said.

"A keepsake," Semih sighed.

"A family keepsake," Hayri insisted. "That's something you can't ever put a price on. Longy never told us that kilim was a family keepsake."

"Didn't I though!" Süleyman protested. "For a whole month I said the same thing to you, and to Semih too. And it was you suggested we swipe it and make a deal of it at the Grand Bazaar. Now, wasn't it?"

"Well, what if I did?" Hayri flared up. "How was I to know Aunt Zare would take sick? If we'd known. . ."

"Would we ever have done such a thing?" Semih said.

"And now, we can't even sell these birds," Süleyman wailed. "People will snap up an old kilim, but they won't buy a single bird."

"So much the worse for them!" Semih burst out. "Turds, that's what they are. They'll see!"

The helicopter that had passed above us a while ago, going in the direction of Firuzköy, was now returning. It was flying so low we could see the men inside.

"Look," Süleyman cried. "Look at the pilots!"

We all gazed up as the helicopter went swiftly by. Tuğrul and his friends also had their heads in the air.

"Well, Longy?" I said. "What happened afterwards?"

"I'd gone crazy, Abi," he began again. "Plum crazy. You see, it was with the money we'd got from the kilim that we bought all our cages. My mum, she rose before my eyes, sick to death because of us. . . Well, I

29

went mad. The minarets of Valide Mosque were whirling round and round, everything went black, and all I saw was that bearded zealot, that hadji stamping away on my cages, a savage beast. Before I knew it, I had hurtled down the steps of the mosque and was at the fellow's throat. I don't know how they got him out of my clutches. I even had my teeth in him."

"They took Longy to a hospital," Semih explained. "But that same night, with God's help, he slipped the collar."

"Another boy there showed me where they'd put away my clothes," Süleyman said. "A good boy, I owe him a lot. . ." He clenched his teeth. "I'm going to kill that hadji," he said with venom. "I swear I will!"

"Don't mind him, Abi," Semih said. "He's in a temper now, so he's talking like this. Just let's get some money from these birds and he won't kill anyone."

"But I will!" Süleyman shook his fists, his eyes bulging. "See if I don't!"

"You mustn't believe him, Abi," Hayri broke in. "He wouldn't kill a fly. Why, if it weren't for us, he'd let all these birds here go free, all of them! He's that soft-hearted, is Longy."

"The birds, yes. I would set them free, but the hadji I'm going to kill. And right there, in Eminönü Square too. And I'll set fire to the body, yes, in front of Valide Mosque."

"No, no, Abi, he's just letting off steam," Semih said with a warning look at Süleyman, as though to say he should not talk like that in front of everyone.

"Why should I hide from him?" Süleyman said, not at all put out. "What Allah knows, why should I hide from his creatures? I'll kill that bigot, and before the winter is over too!"

"Kill him then," Semih cried, exasperated. "Kill him and rot in prison the rest of your life, so Aunt Zare falls really sick this time and dies of grief."

"I can't help it," Süleyman maintained. "Let her die. She needn't have been so poor, that Kurdish Zare. Even if it kills her, I'll still kill that hadji."

"It's Allah who decides whether a person shall be poor or not," Hayri reproved him.

"Piffle!" Süleyman scoffed. "As though Allah had money and was doling it out!"

"Shut up," Semih snapped. "Don't start talking like a heathen."

"Well, I am a heathen," Süleyman retorted coldly.

Hayri turned to me. "Don't mind him, Abi. He's just spoofing. He's not a heathen. He and his family are just Kurdish."

"But I *am* a heathen," Süleyman persisted. "I'm glad to be a heathen. There's nothing better."

"Oh, go fuck yourself!" Semih cried. "You're really drivelling now. Abi, don't you pay any attention to him."

The falcon had drawn quite near. It was flying above the Municipal Beach to the left of the plane tree. But suddenly it glided swiftly off in the direction of the wood and in no time it was lost to sight.

Süleyman glared at Tuğrul's group.

"There now, Abi," he said, shaking his head despondently. "That's how bad luck sticks to you. All because of those fellows staring as though they want to eat us."

"Let them stare. What does it matter?"

31

"Yes, but. . ."

"They're not doing anything to you."

"But they mean to."

"How d'you know?"

"From their eyes," Süleyman said. "They've got that evil shifty look which. . . As though we were enemies. . . Just let them try something! I swear I'll give them a good lesson." He raised his voice. "So help me God, I'll do to them worse than what I did to the hadji."

Semih went on scanning the skies for a time, but there was no sign of the falcon. Süleyman, mad with rage, began to rush about, opening and closing the cages, tugging at the decoy birds, fussing with the clap-net, uprooting tall thistles and planting them in the thicket in front of the net. Then he came across a thistle stalk on which a large yellow flower still held out and he jammed it right in the centre of the thicket.

The three boys returned to their business of trapping the small birds, although the cages were full to bursting and the birds could not even flap their wings any longer but were stacked inside, squirming, one on top of the other, their wings sticking out of the wires.

And still Süleyman persisted in cramming fresh birds into the cages.

"Let them die," he muttered as he rammed in another half-dozen. "It's not my fault. The sin lies with the people of Istanbul, and for their sins this town will turn into another place like Van."

"Like Van, Istanbul will be," Semih concurred. "Worse. . . That's what Allah will do to Istanbul. In the old times, people were kind. Old-time bird-catchers would sell more than a thousand birds in one day for 'fly and be free'. You know that apartment building they call the birdman's house? They say the owner was a bird-catcher just like us. In those days, bird-catchers would dispose of five full cages in one day and no further than Valide Mosque. It's true there weren't so many motorcars then. . ."

"Look here," I expostulated, "they're going to die if you go on cramming them into those cages."

"Of course they'll die," Hayri said, hunching his shoulders and thrusting his hands between his thighs. "They'll die, and then you'll see what'll befall this Istanbul town. An earthquake, that's what! Such an earthquake, not a single house will remain standing. All the buildings will topple to the ground. And the motorcars, they'll be shattered too, broken into a hundred thousand pieces."

"What a shame," Süleyman sighed. "I'll be sorry to see Istanbul destroyed. But it's the fault of the people. They shouldn't be so wicked. Istanbul will be ruined, all because of these tiny little birds. Like Van it'll become."

"It wrings my heart only to look at them," Semih said. "It would wring anyone's heart. The town of Van went to rack and ruin because of birds like these. That's what Aunt Zare told us. And there was nothing left there but the wind howling through the ruins."

"No one with a heart could bear to look at these poor little birds," I said.

"But people have no hearts any more, they've forgotten what mercy is. If it wasn't for that kilim. . . But we'll get it back. And Aunt Zare will be happy again. Oh, how pleased she'll be! There isn't anyone in this whole world as kind-hearted as she. Why, if we went to her now, where she lies on her sick bed, and we showed her these birds in their cages, her heart would burn, it would break. She'd do anything, anything, even sell her house, to buy these birds and set them free, set them soaring into the air all together. Oh, how lovely that would be. . ."

"How lovely. . ." Süleyman echoed. "Oh my poor mum. . ." His eyes filled and he turned away.

"Poor, poor Aunt Zare," Hayri said.

Suddenly, Semih fixed his eyes on me in a long calculating gaze.

"Is it true," he asked at last, "that these falcons catch quails, lots of them?"

"Oh yes, they're famous quail hunters."

"How many do they catch in one day?"

"It depends. . . Sometimes the quails are tired, coming a long way from over the Black Sea. Their wings are wet from the rain as they reach Rize town in the night. The people there put lights along the coast, and the weary birds, attracted by the brightness, pile up beneath the lamps. You see, they can't fly any more, their wings are damp, heavy. . . And so the people can easily gather them up."

"Yes, but what about the falcons?" Semih asked.

"Well, falcons hunt during the day. They're very fast and quails are slow, you know. So when a falcon is flown at quails, it hardly ever misses its prey. Skipper Hasan says that falcons don't tire easily. But you've got to train them. A falcon must learn not to fly off on its own once it's flown. It must be taught to bring back the bird it's caught, and without lacerating it too."

"I know the very man for that!" Semih exclaimed. "It's Ali Şah. A wizard for training birds. He lives down

34

in Dolapdere. I'll take my falcon to him, that's what I'll do. Ohhoo, there's no one like him in all the country!"

"Skipper Hasan trained *my* falcon," I said.

"You had a falcon?" Semih cried in excitement. "What happened to it?"

"I set it free."

"Did it catch quails for you too?"

"Oh yes, a great many."

"How much would a quail cost?" Hayri asked.

"Quails are expensive," I said. "Fifteen to twenty-five liras apiece, I should think. I don't quite know, for I never sold the quails my falcon caught."

Süleyman licked his chops.

"Well, what do you know!" he exclaimed.

"What do you know!" Hayri echoed, and he drew a deep sigh.

Just then, Süleyman uttered a cry of joy.

"Look, look!" He was pointing at the sky. "There are three of them now. Three falcons!"

He rushed to get hold of the clap-net's rope. Hayri grabbed the string attached to the decoys and began pulling them up and down for all he was worth.

Until sunset the three boys kept hard at it, their eyes on the falcons circling above, willing them to make a go for the decoy birds. But it was all in vain. A couple of times the falcons swooped down towards the clap-nets, down down down... The boys waited, their hearts beating high, all agog, then suddenly the birds sheered away, high up in the sky once more.

At nightfall they lit a fire in front of their tent and cooked some soup over it in a soot-blackened pot, all three keeping up a running flow of curses on the population of Istanbul, godless, stone-hearted heathens, all of them.

"It's too awful," Semih began again. "My heart bleeds at the sight. Who knows how many of these little birds will be dead by tomorrow morning. O dear. . ."

"Oh dear," Süleyman took up the refrain. "It really pierces a man's heart to see them like that. If only we had another large cage, and also some grain to feed them, maybe they wouldn't die. But like this. . . Tomorrow. . . Oh dear, they'll die. . ."

"They'll die. . ." Hayri mourned.

"Abi. . ." Semih looked hard at me, his sprouting moustache gleaming redly in the firelight. "Abi, you don't say anything, but I know what you're thinking. You're thinking, if you feel so bad about these birds, why do you catch so many of them, why do you crowd them into cages like this, one on top of the other. . . Isn't that so?"

"Well, yes," I admitted.

"Look, Abi, it's our job to hunt these birds, our duty. We're fowlers and we've come here to catch birds. We haven't invented this 'fly and be free' business. It's an old custom that dates from way back. The fowlers catch the birds and the people of Istanbul pay to set them free."

"That's true," I said.

"But now, the way things are, all these birds here won't even live out the night, maybe."

"Maybe they will. You never know. . ."

"Maybe they will," Semih conceded. "But what if we catch another five hundred tomorrow and have to squeeze them into these cages as well?"

36

"That's a poser," I said.

"And how!" There was a long brooding silence.

I looked at the three drooping heads and then I said: "Listen, there's something we can do."

Three heads popped up eagerly.

"I'll give you a hundred liras now," I suggested, "and you can buy a new cage with the money."

"Oh no, we can't," Semih demurred.

"Why not?"

"We can't take your money. Why, we hardly know you!"

"Hardly at all," Süleyman said.

"It's not right," Hayri cried. "We'd be ashamed to do such a thing. We're not beggars."

"No, of course not," I hastened to say. "But you're going to capture that falcon anyway. So I thought I'd give you the money for it in advance."

"Ah then... We're sure to have it here for you tomorrow."

"Before that fellow with the agate eyes arrives..."

"Yes, it must be before," Süleyman said.

We all looked in the direction of Tuğrul's group. They were still crouching there in the darkness, perfectly quiet.

I produced a hundred-lira note and handed it over. The faces of the three boys glowed, and when I rose to go they all three leaped to their feet as though triggered by a single spring.

"Well, so long," I said.

"Tomorrow," Semih said. "Come tomorrow. We'll have the falcon, maybe even three. All real good hunters... The kind that'll bag you a hundred quails a day."

4

For the next couple of days, business prevented me
from going down to Florya Plain. But I was burning to
know whether the boys had captured a falcon.

That morning I was awakened very early by the rat-
a-tat of a scow laden with sand, heading for Ambarli.
The sky was clear, luminous, the sun just about to
appear behind the minarets. Soon, its rays would flare
up over Istanbul. The rumble of the distant city
reached Basinköy in a moaning monotone.

I went out and strolled over to the almond grove.
The trees had already begun to shed their leaves. The
thistle shrubs were alive with thousands of little birds,
twittering away as if all hell had broken loose. It was
incredible how many there were, tiny little birds, yellow, buff, red, honey-coloured, green, blue, myriads,
fluttering from one clump of thistles to another.

"Those years when the thistles are grown tall and
thick. . ."

"Those years when their needles are long and loaded
with flowers. . ."

"When the earth has seen rain in plenty, and snow as
well. . ."

"Then they will throng up in thousands, the small
bright birds, to Florya Plain. . ."

"Then the cages of the fowlers will overflow, all for

38

'fly and be free'..."

And so, in those good years, it was a sight for sore eyes on an autumn day to watch the children of Menekşe and Florya, of Cennet, Yeşilyurt and Şenlik-köy, all spruced up in clean, brand-new clothes, trousers, coats, shirts, shoes, all bought with the fruit of their labour, the money from the sale of the birds they had caught, to see them parade up and down in the more prosperous neighbourhoods of Basinköy and Yeşilköy, showing off to the girls there.

For, when the thistle shrubs are hardy on Florya Plain and their flowers have bloomed all through the summer, then, come the autumn, their seeds are sure to be abundant. And these are the seeds which the little migratory birds are so fond of. That is why they come in thousands, swarming onto Florya Plain, clustering over the thistle stalks, dried up now and glistening with a coppery glow.

It was a wonderful din the birds were making that morning, all in a ferment, a riot of colour on Florya Plain.

In a few minutes, I came to the tent. And what should I find! A dismal silence reigned there and Semih was nowhere to be seen. The long lad's head was wrapped in bandages, his hands cut and bruised, his clothes stained with blood. Hayri's face, too, was scratched, a long gash ran down the arch of his eyebrow and his trousers were in tatters. They did not even lift their heads to greet me, but just sat there glumly, in front of the tent. Tuğrul and his friends, I noticed, were no longer in their usual place.

I squatted down beside them on a patch of turf.

"Well, speak up, whatever's happened to you?"

Süleyman turned to me slowly and gave me a wary look.

"Nothing," he said at last.

"Nothing, really," Hayri supported him.

I glanced at the cages. They were full to bursting. It would have been impossible to squeeze another bird into any one of them. Süleyman caught my look and a trace of joy passed over his face.

"It's a rain of birds today," he said. "You wouldn't believe it! Our arms are aching from pulling those strings, Hayri and me. Just look at those cages!"

No sooner had he spoken than we saw a flight of birds flitting swiftly our way from over the railway station. Right above us, they broke into two groups, and one of the groups came to settle plumb upon the boys' clump of thistles.

"Let them come," Süleyman growled. "What good will it do us? They don't sell. There's nothing we can do with them in this godforsaken town." His face was tense with fury.

"Heathen! That's what Istanbul is, a heathen town." Hayri spat out a huge gob of spittle. "Damned for ever." And he ground his teeth.

"Come now, what happened?" I said pointing to their scratched faces. "And where's Semih?"

"Don't ask," Süleyman said. "He's gone."

"Why's that?"

"He just went away."

With a motion of my head, I indicated the plane tree where Tuğrul had been.

Süleyman clenched his fists. He leaped to his feet, then flopped down again.

"Out with it, Longy," I insisted.

Süleyman gave a short laugh. Then, as though divulging a piece of good news, he said: "We captured your falcon three days ago, as soon as you left."

"Well then. . ."

"It's as if it was waiting for you to go, that bird. The minute you were away, it turned up, right there, over the plane tree. And before we knew it, it had swooped down over the decoy bird and was making away with it. But Semih was quicker. He grabbed the rope and brought the net down in the nick of time. And if I hadn't pounced there in a couple of steps, the falcon would have torn the net and escaped. At that moment, Semih snatched the bird from my hands. . ."

He stopped. There was an uncomfortable silence. Süleyman swallowed. His eyes riveted on my face, his neck longer than ever, he seemed unable to say another word.

I had to press him to go on.

"What is it, Süleyman?" I asked. "What's wrong?"

He was sweating now. The veins in his long neck twitched.

"You know what he said, that Semih, the minute he got hold of that bird?" he blurted out, then broke off again.

"How should I know? Tell me."

He made a big effort, while Hayri just sat there, mute, staring at the ground.

"You know what he said, he said this bird's mine. I like it too much to give it to anyone. . . Yes indeed, that's exactly what he said. . ."

"And then?"

Hayri lifted his head. "That Semih's no good, he hasn't got a spark of honour in him." He flung the words out very quickly, almost shouting. Then he fell silent, his head hanging, his face crimson. The next instant, he jumped to his feet. "It's such a rotten thing to do," he murmured, standing there, quite at a loss. "A crying shame, that's what it is, a crying shame!" And he sank back, his knees huddled to his chin.

Then Süleyman spoke again. "I tried to argue with him. For heaven's sake, Semih, I said, you can't do things like that! We've already taken the money for this bird from that kind man, haven't we? It belongs to him now..."

"The shame of it, that anyone calling himself a man should do such a thing..." Hayri said.

"Semih, I said..." Süleyman's voice was trembling. "Man, how can you take this bird for yourself when we've already sold it and spent the money?"

"Ugh, it's too sickening!" Hayri cried.

"If we don't give that good man his bird, it'll mean there's no trusting anyone any more," Süleyman pursued. "So I said to him... Listen, Semih, I said, we'll catch another one and that one will be yours. And he said to me... Ah, it's too awful... He said, we'll give that man the next bird we catch, this one's my very own, my kismet... For shame, I said, is there no honesty left in this world? And while we were arguing, those boys over there, you know, the ones with the agate eyes..."

"Agate," Hayri hissed, "agate..."

"They were watching us, those agate eyes wide, goggling, like this..." Süleyman's eyes bulged from their sockets. "You wouldn't believe it, Abi, you know why they sat there all those days, watching us?"

I'd been wondering about that too.

"Did you find out, then?"

"They were waiting to see when we would decide to wring the little birds' necks and eat them. Imagine! Roast them to make a meal! Hungry we may be, yes, but we'd rather die of hunger than roast those little birds and eat them..."

Their big secret was out. But now Süleyman bitterly regretted having spoken like this. Striving to change the subject, he spluttered on. "That hundred liras you gave us... For fifty, we bought another cage. We had to, there was no help for it... And Semih took the rest of the money. He wouldn't let us touch it."

"You mean, you couldn't buy anything to eat?"

"Oh, but we did, we did! We bought lots of bread. Today, we really had our fill, olives, bread, cheese... Yummy! Hayri went and got the bread from Menekşe, freshly baked... Warm, just out of the oven, oooh, it burned my hand, ooooh, it was so good..." He closed his eyes. "Wasn't it, Hayri? I have a swollen belly, I ate so much. Such a good feed we had today, wasn't it, Hayri? That baker always gives Hayri the freshest of his loaves and, even if there's no bread left, he keeps a loaf hidden for us inside the oven. And in exchange we bring him five large greenfinches every day... Warm... Isn't that so, Hayri?"

Hayri raised his head. There was a hard bitter expression on his face and when his eyes met mine I saw they were full of tears.

"Warm..." he murmured, and that was all he had to say.

"Well, we had our meal today," Süleyman said.

Hayri smiled sadly.

In my turn, I felt an urgent need to change the

43

subject.

"But what happened afterwards?" I said.

Süleyman clutched at my question as at a lifebuoy.

"Afterwards... Well, Abi, Semih went into the tent and brought out a cage full of birds. Then he let all the birds out and put the falcon in instead. The bird had clawed and scratched him and he was bleeding badly by this time. All red with blood he was, isn't that so, Hayri?"

Hayri's three-cornered eyes were more than ever like two triangles.

"All red," he said.

"Then, after he'd got the falcon safely in the cage..."

5

~~~

The falcon's chest was bluish grey, its beak hooked
and strong, its wings a chestnut colour. It was a very
large bird with huge bright eyes that shone fiercely in
their sockets. Crammed into that long cage, it had
tried to fling its wings open and one of them had
remained sticking out of the wires, while the other
was folded back.

After making sure the falcon was secure in the cage,
Semih, not even pausing to wipe the blood from his
face and hands, marched up to the six boys under the
poplar and planted himself in front of Tuğrul. For a
while, they faced each other in silence, the six sturdy,
already grown boys on one side, Semih all by himself
on the other.

Semih was the first to speak.

"So what the hell?" he burst out, clenching his fists.
"For days you've been staring your eyes out as though
you wanted to eat us. What the hell, haven't you ever
seen human beings before?"

"Human beings, yes," Tuğrul sneered.

"Hell is where your own father's gone to," Hüseyin
said.

"Don't go picking a quarrel with these hoodoos,"
Erol the fisher boy advised his companions. His clothes
were stuck with fish scales and he reeked of fish from

45

yards away.

"Hoodoo yourself! And your father, and all your ancestors," Semih retorted, bracing his shoulders, fists at the ready. "You agate-eyed, ill-omened dog! Ever since we've been here, you've fixed those nasty eyes of yours on us, spying on us, that's what, like any vulgar slut, Menekşe street sluts!"

"Who's spying on you?" Hüseyin said.

"We're just here to see how you'll soon be dying of hunger," Fisher Erol said. "With all those birds that you'll never be able to sell. . ."

"Why, your mouths stink of hunger already!" Tuğrul said.

At that, Long Süleyman moved to Semih's side.

"We've got birds, yes, and plenty of them," he said. "What the hell is it to you, you bunch of mollycoddles, if we do die of hunger? Will your mother burn henna for us to dye her you-know-where? A lot of candles she'll be needing, thirty-six at least. . ."

"More, much more," Semih laughed. "The way they're made, their mothers, it's three hundred and eighty candles they'll have to burn for all that henna to fill their you-know-where!"

Stunned at the abuse being heaped upon them, the others cast about for some stronger insults but found themselves unable to hit upon anything to equal tough Semih's inventive aspersions.

Semih on his part went on, non-stop, with a string of abuse.

Tuğrul swallowed and swallowed again. He tried to speak.

"You. . . But you. . . You. . ." he stammered.

Suddenly, Semih stopped. "What about us?" he

46

challenged him. He was obviously eager to add fuel to the flame.

"You... When you're too hungry to bear it any more, you're going to wring those little birds' necks and gorge yourselves."

Semih hooted with laughter.

"So we are! We'll gorge ourselves and good for us. We caught them and we'll eat them. Right here we'll light a fire and when the embers are all aglow we'll roast them. Yum! Who knows how tasty they are, these goldfinches, these greenfinches when they're roasted. Yummy, yummy!"

He smacked his lips.

"It's to please ourselves we came hunting here. Of course we're going to eat them."

And he smacked his lips again with relish.

Longy and Hayri smacked their lips too, just like him. The others were dumbfounded.

Then Tuğrul snickered: "They're going to eat those tiny little birds! Shame! Boo..."

"Boo," Hüseyin hooted.

"Beasts," Fisher Erol cried. "Eating tiny little creatures! Boo!"

"We *will* eat them. Good for us!"

The squabbling went on and on, back and forth, until they ran out of insults and their voices were hoarse. Then, all of a sudden, no one knew how it started, the two groups were at each other's throats and a regular fight was in full swing in the middle of Florya Plain. Though they were three against six, the tough boys from Fatih soon got the better of the molly-coddles. They'd gone through many another fight and squabble in their lives. It all ended in piercing screams

47

that came from under the poplar and could be heard all the way from Basinköy and Menekşe and even from Şenlikköy.

Semih had drawn his knife and was stalking about Florya Plain, brandishing it, while the six boys, crazed with fear, scattered, shrieking in terror, running for their lives.

6

~~~

"Yes, Abi, that's exactly how it happened. Semih just spat after them, after those milksops, he spat three times, stuffed the knife back into his pocket and went and washed his face at that fountain there. Then he took the falcon out of the cage and tied a string to its foot and simply went away. He left without a single word either to me or to Hayri. Tell me, Abi, is that a thing to do to a friend? It's not right."

"Oh, what does it matter?" Hayri said impatiently.

"But how can it not matter?" Süleyman's eyes were wide and puzzled, his neck stretched longer and longer. "If Semih can do a thing like that, then there's no one you can trust in this world any more."

"Semih will come back," Hayri stated with conviction. "See if he doesn't."

"I know he will, yes, Semih's not a heel, but. . . But to turn his back on us, to leave like that, without a word!"

"Shut up!" Hayri cried, exasperated. "Lay off, will you? I'm telling you he'll be back."

Süleyman was quelled. "Of course he will," he faltered.

"And I'm going to catch another falcon for Abi tomorrow."

"Never mind about that," I said. "It's all right. If you

49

can't catch it. . ."

"What? Of course we must!" Süleyman cried. "It would be really shabby of us if we didn't."

"We'd be so ashamed of ourselves," Hayri said.

"In that case, children, let me give you another hundred liras. You can buy a couple of new cages and if there's anything left over. . ."

"No, no," Süleyman protested.

"We can't. . ." Hayri cried.

They were as determined not to accept the money as I was to make them take it. After a long argument, I emerged as the winner and I shoved the money into Hayri's pocket.

"Your bird will be ready here for you tomorrow," Süleyman vowed. "Cross my heart and hope to die."

"Tomorrow," Hayri said. "I'll tie thirty or forty decoys around the thistles, sixty if necessary, so the falcons can't fail to catch the scent. They'll be down at them in no time."

"Good," I said. "And I'm going to Menekşe. There are some old fowlers there who may be able to give me tips as to how to sell these birds of prey. You boys are good at catching them, but you've no idea at all how to sell them."

"That's true," they confessed.

7

~~~

It was indeed a rain of birds over Florya Plain that morning. All about me, as I walked down to the coffee house at Menekşe, hundreds of tiny twittering birds were sputtering over the thistle shrubs like hot popcorn. Where did they come from in such great numbers, and, after staying here from September to the middle of December, where did they go to? To what new distant thistle fields? Towards the end of December there are no thistles left on Florya Plain. Stormy winds, the fierce *poyraz* from the north, the black nor'wester, and also the *lodos* from the south, which whips the sea into a white foaming mass, will have uprooted them, tossing them this way and that and scattering their seeds over the earth. What a magician nature is, what prodigies she performs! All these tiny birds, each one no bigger than a thumb, who knows how far they will travel, what mountains and steppes, what seas, what deserts they will traverse? Who knows where they will nest at last to lay their eggs? The human mind boggles before the wonders of nature. These flecks of brilliant colour, how she scatters them in the skies, soaring, plunging, sheering, a sparkling flashing turmoil. . .

I came to the coffee house. Fishing boats were moored under the little bridge in front of it. There I found Mahmut.

Mahmut is a native of Menekşe, born and bred here. He knows these purlieus of Istanbul like the palm of his hand, Menekşe, Çekmece, Ambarli, the Long-Grotto, the lake, the seas and seamarks. He can reel off the names of half a dozen of those little autumn birds, detailing the colour of their plumage, their character-istic call notes, the shape of their bills, their eyes. . . Mahmut doesn't show his age, but by my reckoning he must be sixty or so. Some days, when he's in a black mood, you can see him ambling along the seashore, his hands clasped behind his back, refusing to speak to anyone, and this can last from dawn to dusk.

"Hello, Mahmut," I hailed him.

"Why, hey there, hello!" He gave me a questioning look.

"Let's take a turn Yeşilköy way," I said. "I've got things to ask you."

"All right," he said, and his face beamed. It was like an explosion of joy. I've never met another who laughs like Mahmut, from the heart's core, forcing you to share his gladness. Suddenly, I felt light and sunny, relieved of the grime, the rust of Istanbul town, the evil, the cupidity that made people so beastly to each other. May you have a long life, Mahmut, my friend, enduring as this earth, may you ever be here with your humble heartfelt laughter springing from the very veins in your body. Bless you, Mahmut, my friend. . .

Strangely enough, people who laugh like this always have very white teeth that gleam like pearls. . .

"I'll bet you're at it again," he said. "You want me to give you some names of birds and fishes."

Right away, he was ticking off fish names, unusual

fish no one had ever heard of. All the way from Menekşe to Florya, he went on teaching me names of fishes and describing their colours and habits.

"Wait," I said at last. "I'll have to write all this down so I won't forget it. But some other day."

"Write it down, you must," he said. "Write down all that Mahmut tells you, Mahmut the bard of the denizens of the deep. That's our job, to celebrate the fish of the sea."

"Tell me, have you really caught all those fish you were just telling me about?"

"Not likely!" he said. "Some of those fish don't even frequent the seas around here. But I have seen every one of them, those I've been telling you about, because I've fished in the Mediterranean in my time, all the way to Algeria."

"And what about those birds you keep describing?"

The smile froze on his face.

"Those I hunted, every one of them. Would that I hadn't. . ."

And he was launched on the subject of birds.

Ever since ancient Byzantium, and even further back . . . In those days, the land stretching beyond the Old Walls of the city up to Florya Plain was all woods and fields and thistle shrubs, with not a single house in sight. The little autumn birds would come not like this, not like now, but in hordes, clouding the sky, like swarms of butterflies. . . If you happened to be sitting by one of the thistle shrubs and you rose suddenly, you would find yourself engulfed by hundreds of those tiny birds, their wings brushing your face and hands. It was like standing under a shower of birds. There was a blue bird then, it doesn't come anymore, the species must

53

have died out. So tiny it was, hardly larger than a thumb. Oh well, maybe bigger than that, a man's brain is not a machine, it may sometimes remember a small thing as large and what is big as tiny... Anyway, this bird was a rich blue, with large black eyes and a lovely graceful bill, a shimmering blue, flawless, that flooded a man's face, his very soul, in a torrent of light. The whole world was drowned in this rich blueness. Why, those birds even made the night blue, and the moonlight too...

There was no village then, at Şenlikköy, only vegetable gardens and blindfolded horses working the treadmills among the green lushness. And always that rain of blue birds... They would perch on your shoulders, your head, your arms, so many of them you looked like you had turned into a blue statue.

"In all the years of my life, I've never come across a bird so close to people, so warm, so trusting, more human than a human being."

"Did you catch these blue birds too and sell them for 'fly and be free' in front of mosques?"

"Never! I didn't have the heart to do that. They were so soft, such a velvety blue. No, the ones I caught for 'fly and be free' were the chaffinches, the coal titmice, the goldfinches... They're small too, yes, but sturdy, whereas the blue bird is frail, light as a feather, as if like a butterfly it might dissolve into dust at a touch... No, never, not once did I sell one of those blue birds for 'fly and be free and meet me at the gates of Paradise'. They were my very own sacred birds, the blue ones. It was for me, perhaps, that they came this way, for Mahmut's sake... I hardly dared touch them, even in a caress..."

In those days, thousands of birds would be captured on Florya Plain and taken to Istanbul to be sold in front of the mosques of Eyup, Valide, Sultan Ahmed, Mihrimah, Fatih, and before Haghia Sophia too. "Fly little bird, free as the air, and meet me at the gates of Paradise..." The cages would be taken by storm, people would vie with each other to buy the birds. Why, the fowlers could never catch enough to meet the needs of Istanbul town!

And before churches too, and synagogues, every day, thousands of birds were released from their cages with prayers and invocations, and their joyful flight to freedom would be followed with pride and hope by their deliverers.

Once, Mahmut had tied coloured threads to the feet of a whole cageful of birds before he sold them, different coloured threads, yellow, red, blue, green...

"I sold them for 'fly and be free' in front of Valide Mosque, all those tagged birds. In one instant, the sky over the mosque, over Eminönü and Karaköy was full of them. Then I went back and set my clap-net over there, where the wood is now. At that time, the place was a jungle of thistles. And after a while, in the afternoon, what should I see! Six of the tagged birds right there, back in my clap-net! In one week I had retrieved three hundred and six of them. And when, three years later, I discovered another one in my net, I was mad with joy."

In those days, fowling was a lucrative affair for children. One hesitates to say that people were better then, yet, who knows, maybe they were different. Maybe they liked birds better. Maybe they were more soft-hearted, more loving, more easily moved to pity.

55

Maybe they were closer to nature, who knows...
People nowadays don't give a damn if little birds die in
their cages. People don't even go to church or to the
synagogue any more, or perhaps only from Sunday to
Sunday, and merely a sprinkling at that, or to attend a
funeral now and then. As for those roundbeards emerg-
ing from mosques, wearing black berets, all with harsh
angry countenances, grinding their teeth, those surly,
deathlike zealots so unbecoming to the laughing face
of the great Süleymaniye Mosque, it isn't from them
one can expect pity for little birds shut up in a cage,
not theirs the faith for "fly and be free"... Heigh-ho, a
bloody world it is now... Perhaps in Eyup, among the
humble poor of Eyup there is still some compassion
left. Maybe also up in Taksim Square... Taksim is the
most populous part of the town. Wouldn't there be
some, among the crowds that always throng the
square, just a few with still a modicum of humanity
who, for a trifling sum, will take pride and joy in set-
ting little birds free? Such a sight it is when those birds
soar joyously up into the sky...

"Yes, if there's any hope left, it's in Taksim and
Eyup."

"So charity is dead, is it?"

"Dead?" Mahmut said. "No, not dead, but in
trouble, stranded somewhere or other."

"Is that what you think? Where then?"

A bright smile lit up Mahmut's face and I thought,
perhaps that's where charity is now, right there in
Mahmut's genial laughter, in the fullness of his heart.
Who knows, maybe...

"The birds, too, have gone away," Mahmut said
suddenly.

We fell silent. The birds are gone now. And with the birds. . . It's no use. . . Even the birds are gone.

These sullen, shifty-eyed zealots with berets on their heads, who emerge from the mosques as though having waged a mighty battle with God, as though whatever light there was in their faces has remained inside, are these the faithful, these men under whose angry tread the earth seems to split, these the believers? No wonder the birds have gone, left this place long ago. . .

And in Taksim Square, those people jostling each other, spitting loudly all over the place, blowing their noses with their fingers and then wiping off the snot onto the nearest tree trunk, the men with sickly faces, the garishly painted women, the surly choleric countenances, the hostile eyes, each man an enemy to the other, each ready to spring at the other's throat, to gouge out the other's eyes. . . And those who are afraid, and those who are ashamed, and those who are always bragging, I, I, I. . . Those stinking creatures, human beings? No wonder the birds have gone. . . And with the birds. . .

"Maybe in front of factories, as the workers disperse. . . Maybe at the Vegetable Market the Kurdish *hamals* might. . . Those Kurds, they can hardly speak our tongue, but they dote on birds. . ."

Maybe somewhere, in some corner or other, there are a few people left still generous enough to buy birds and set them free. Who knows, maybe. . .

Go ahead then, Long Süleyman, go ahead triangular-eyed, taciturn, angry Hayri. Load up your cages full of birds! Human beings are so unpredictable. Who knows but that in Taksim Square they may be seized with a

57

sudden frenzy and start queueing to buy your birds, and not only one but five, ten, twenty apiece, so as to fling them up into the air. In no time, the cages will be empty and your pockets full of wads of money. How bitterly Semih will regret having abandoned you, how remorseful, how ashamed he'll be. For man is a strange creature, truly unpredictable, who knows but you might hit upon one of his good days. . .

8

~~~

For a few days I kept away from the tent beside the poplar. What if the boys had not been able to capture that falcon... I was a thousand times sorry I had suggested they should catch it for me.

Then, one evening, I felt I could not stay away any longer. I was burning to know what had happened to those boys. Had they given up? Had they caught more and more of those little birds?

Indeed, from my window I could see the birds coming in greater numbers than ever. Florya Plain was one big patchwork of many flickering colours, now red, now yellow, green, orange, blue... The muffled rumbling of the distant city merged with the chittering of birds that flitted in swarms from thistle to thistle. The dry copper-coloured thistles were covered with birds, swaying lightly in the air.

That night, the sky was laden with stars. The starlight cast a dull shimmer over the gently rippling sea. The warm scent of pines drifted in from the wood and mingled with the odour of brine and iodine.

I was cheered to see a small fire burning in front of the tent. So the boys had not gone away, they were still at it, holding their ground...

There was something odd in the way they greeted me. They were not exactly cold, but obviously far from pleased to see me. Hayri did not even look up.

Süleyman cleared his throat several times. He seemed to have trouble speaking. Hurriedly, he spread a newspaper in front of the fire.

"Sit down, Abi," he said morosely. "Welcome. . ."

I sat on the newspaper and he dropped down beside me. Hayri was still standing.

"Come and sit here, Hayri," I said.

He crouched down to my right, averting his face.

"Welcome," he murmured.

Our eyes fixed on the fire, we did not speak for a while.

"Abi," Süleyman blurted out suddenly, "that friend of yours, Mahmut Abi, he came here, you know. He talked with us. He asked about the birds, how we were doing. . . He's a good man."

"That he is," I agreed. "Mahmut's the best fellow in the world."

"Listen, Abi," Süleyman began again. "Listen. . ." He was talking very quickly now, as though afraid the words would be stolen from his mouth before he had time to utter them. "Ah Abi, we couldn't catch your bird. It's like those big birds have a grudge against us. They used to come again and again, but every time they came, we chased them away, we humiliated them by not catching even one, by bagging all these small birds instead. So they were offended and took themselves off in a huff. Wouldn't you do the same if you were in their place, if you'd been driven away time after time? Wouldn't you, if you had a spark of pride, wouldn't you go away and never come back again? Wouldn't you, Abi?"

"I suppose so," I said.

60

"Well then. . . Those birds too have gone away."

"It happens they disappear sometimes. I shouldn't worry," I said.

"Look, Abi, as God's my witness, we fixed maybe a hundred decoys here. . ."

"A hundred," Hayri repeated without lifting his head.

"One day, for a whole day from morning till dark, there were seven of them up there, above that poplar, seven falcons hovering wing to wing, not even flying, just floating on the breeze, and we down here, pulling at those decoys, up, down, up, down, and would you believe it, not one of those falcons made the slightest move to attack them. They did not even bend sideways to look at the fluttering decoys! And then, in the afternoon, Hayri couldn't bear it any more. . ."

Süleyman paused, looking at me insistently.

"No one could bear it," I said.

"So Hayri looked at those birds and blasted out a bellyful of curses. He called them turds and carrion crows and all sorts of bad names. He swore and swore . . ."

"So what?" Hayri flung out savagely. "I cursed, I swore, so what?"

"You did right," I said.

Hayri gave me a wary look as if to say, are you mocking me now?

"Of course you did right," I repeated. "There's nothing to be done with such dirty stubborn birds but swear at them well and good."

Hayri seemed more at ease now.

"But after that, the birds went away," Süleyman persisted. "They couldn't put up with all that cursing.

61

They flew off and never came back. Hayri's not one for talking much, you know, but there are few people in Istanbul town who know so many swear words."

"Very few," Hayri said.

"He learned all those swear words from a real master, Ismail, a former wrestler, who is now a fisherman in Samatya."

"Ismail the Laz, from Samatya," Hayri said proudly.

"One would have to be made of stone to take all those curses lying down. How could the birds not be offended?"

"Impossible..."

"So they've gone away," Süleyman concluded, still with that mortified look on his face.

"Oh, they'll be back," Hayri cried. "They'll soon have forgotten all about it."

He rose and flung his arms out wide.

"Like this they'll swoop down on the decoys! And like this I'll capture them, yes..."

And silently he enacted the scene, the swift plunge of the falcon, the clap-net snapping over it, himself seizing the struggling bird as it clawed at his hands and stuffing it into the cage at last. Still without a word, he slumped down again.

"We're very sorry, Abi," Süleyman said. "We haven't kept our word, we haven't got your falcon. But they'll come back, those birds. Sooner or later..."

"Yes," I said. "Birds forget quickly. Sooner or later..."

"They'll be back," Hayri stated with conviction.

"And we'll catch them this time, we will..."

"You mustn't worry so much," I said. "If you don't catch them, well, never mind."

"But we have to, Abi," Hayri countered stiffly. "We're not beggars, or swindlers either."

"Why, what kind of talk is that?" I protested. "Of course not!"

Süleyman hastened to change the subject.

"Mahmut Abi. . ." he began.

How, in the dark, did I guess that Hayri was much more at his ease now? He did not speak, and I could hardly make out his features in the light of the flickering fire.

Süleyman got up and collected an armful of dry brushwood from the foot of the barbed wire fence. He threw the wood onto the fire which blazed up. Hayri also went to get some wood and soon they had built up quite a pile beside the fire.

"Now we're all right," Hayri said.

For a long time we sat there before the fire, silent, the three of us, each one alone with his thoughts. Then Long Süleyman began to talk. And suddenly Hayri was talking too, Hayri the taciturn one, talking twenty to the dozen. That's how it is, sometimes, with close-mouthed people. Once started, there's no stopping them.

The whiteness of the dawn sea hit the topmost branches of the great plane tree in front of the Municipal Beach. The crest of the tree was bathed in brightness and from there a stream of light flowed out into the plain.

Over Istanbul city, the sky was flame-red. The sun was about to rise, and soon the leaden domes of the mosques would turn pale. From Ambarli way came the throb of an early motorboat. The two boys had fallen asleep, still sitting, their heads drooping to their chests.

The flames had died out and the fire was crumbling into ashes now. In their cages the birds must have been asleep too, though a faint beating of wings sounded now and then from the cramped cage at the foot of the poplar. The dawn breeze was blowing gently, coming from everywhere, from the woods, the sea, the lake, filling the whole world with gladness and making a man feel all cleansed and pure inside, light as a feather, ready to take wing.

9

Ali Şah lives in Dolapdere. And this Dolapdere is by far the most enchanting quarter of Istanbul, a bustling hodgepodge of a place. Istanbul is immense, the city seems to stretch on and on infinitely, its populace teems like ants, but the limits of this multiformity, this hugeness, are well-defined. Dolapdere is small, but it is a universe in itself, boundless in its variety. One can confidently assert that it is unique in the world. A labyrinth of streets and alleys, of shanties, brothels and ill-famed hotels, yet chaste and pure at heart. . . Dirty enough to engulf all of Istanbul, yet its dwellings scoured clean as a new penny. . . A pageant of humanity, garage mechanics, odd-job men who can repair oil lamps, sailors' lanterns, people who can produce a brand-new bicycle out of a couple of old wheels, rebuild a car, devise some new kind of outboard motor or even an original watercraft. . . Cobblers hammering in hobnails, weavers, lottery-men and people drawing for lots, vendors of black-market cigarettes, hard-drinking carousers who know how to hold their drink, blind-drunk boozers – you can run across all kinds in Dolapdere. All the failures, the wash-outs of the universe seem to have taken refuge here and found an anchorage. In Dolapdere, vice and turpitude, corruption and treachery are rampant, but so are friendship and love. Indeed, it is a magic town. Whatever his origin, whether he comes from the mansion of a bey or the tent of a gypsy, the man who has once lived in Dolapdere will never again escape from its slime and hurly-burly, not if you offer him the whole world. Kurd or gypsy, English, French, Laz, Turk or Turcoman, Arab or Persian, once a man has settled here, wild horses cannot drag him away.

All kinds of languages are spoken in Dolapdere. Swarthy gypsies, fair-haired immigrants, tall Kurds, beautiful-eyed Georgians, and countless others have brought with them their thousand and one songs, their thousand and one dialects. Not in the whole of Istanbul is there a place to match Dolapdere. In fact, I defy anyone to show me another like it in the whole world.

Take the autumn of 1943 when Zühre, that Dolapdere beauty, with her waist so slim and her long lustrous black hair reaching down to her ankles – the women of Dolapdere have the loveliest hair – when Zühre, bronze-skinned, blue-eyed, won the belly dance championship. Dancing for three days and three nights in Kasimpaşa Square, with God only knows how many undulations of the belly a minute, she wrested the first rank from the famed Sulukule gypsies and made the whole of Sulukule and the neighbourhood of the Old Walls burst with vexation like an overripe red watermelon.

That's how renowned Dolapdere is! And its most renowned resident is undoubtedly Ali Şah. Of course, there is Rüstem the fiddler, with his performing bears, and Halim the Black Sea viol player, and Gülizar the belle of easy virtue, but no one in Dolapdere has yet attained Ali Şah's repute. Not even the most noted gypsy chiefs of Sulukule can measure up to Ali Şah for his many talents, his staunchness, his courage, his loyalty. Ali Şah always girds himself with a wide red sash, as in the days when he was chief of a gypsy tribe in Edirne. He speaks with an Albanian accent, starting with the "a bé moré" so typical of Albanians. Maybe he does come from Albania, but no one can tell, just as no one can tell where the wolf's lair is. Who knows when he came strolling into Dolapdere, as nonchalantly as though he owned the place, and then, the moment he was settled, became the most respected personality there, everybody's mentor, whom you could trust and tell all your troubles to. As for his gypsy clan, one fine day, so the story goes, he got bored of being a chief. Here, he told the clan as though handing over his old coat, take back your trust, I can't go on with this task, goodbye and bless you all... And so he took himself off. Where he went after that, what countries he roamed, what adventures befell him, God only knows.

One has only to ask something of Ali Şah and he will do it for you, regardless of what it costs him. Not that anyone would dare approach him with a trifling matter. Ali Şah knows this, and that is why he never turns away someone who comes knocking at his door.

And now, our Semih, the one who ran off with the falcon, leaving his friends in the lurch with hundreds of unsaleable birds on Florya Plain, hungry, penniless, that same Semih is going straight to Ali Şah. How does Semih know of Ali Şah, you'll ask. Ah, but that's Semih for you, a lad who has scoured every street and back alley of Istanbul town, who has worn his soles

67

out in every gutter, on every pavement...

Ali Şah wears a long grizzling yellow moustache, and every morning he rubs and twists this moustache with almond oil until it is shining bright. In his younger days, he used to dye his moustache with henna. It was flame-red then, majestic, awe-inspiring, but it is two years now since he gave up this practice. Ali Şah always goes about with two revolvers thrust into that red sash of his, and no policeman has ever apprehended him for this. Indeed, no one, police or civilian, would dare take issue with Ali Şah. Just let someone try and all the pickpockets and thieves of Dolapdere, the cutthroats and toughs, the local lads and girls would fly at him in a holy rage and make Istanbul town too hot for him.

Semih will go to Ali Şah and say to him, train this falcon for me, train it well so it'll bag a hundred quails a day, even two hundred... Yes, that's what Semih will do. No one else in the world understands the language of birds like Ali Şah. He'll work on a falcon a week, or maybe a fortnight, at the most a month, and in the end he'll have made of that falcon an Azrael for quails.

Afterwards, Semih will make straight for Kilyos village and set up tent on the rise where the Coast Guard station stands. And perhaps, if he feels like it and if they are of a mind to patch up the quarrel, he'll allow Long Süleyman and Hayri to come too. For it is there that quails drop onto the shore, exhausted, after travelling across the wide sea, coming from far-off lands beyond the Black Sea. It always rains as they cross the water and their wings are wet and heavy. Then is the time to fly the falcon. Like lightning it'll swoop over

68

the quails, but it'll never eat its prey, only wait for Semih. And Semih will run and bag the quails... If they are reconciled, then Long Süleyman and Hayri too will gather quails on the shore, fat juicy quails, a hundred, maybe two hundred in one day. They will fill plastic bags with them, jump into the *dolmuş** that goes from Kilyos to Taksim Square and then make for the butcher shops behind the Flower Market. The quails will sell for two and a half liras apiece. A hundred quails will make two hundred and fifty liras, two hundred will be five hundred, two hundred and fifty, six hundred and twenty-five liras, isn't that right? With quails it's not like with those miserable little birds. There's always a ready market for quails, you deliver them and pocket the cash, as easy at that! And who knows, a quail may be selling for ten or twenty liras these days...

Don't imagine that Semih will hunt quails with his falcon only. Oh no! There are those long nets fishermen hang up to dry on the wharves at Rumelihisar. That's where Semih plans to pilfer a net of two. He has often done this in the past, selling off the nets to fishermen in another part of the town, telling them, my father went to sea and never returned, his boat leaked, a storm blew up, these are his nets... If they make it up, Semih, Hayri and Long Süleyman... And why shouldn't they? There's been no blood shed between them... This isn't the first time Semih has played a dirty trick on them, not by a long shot! Well, anyway, they'll hang those nets along the shore of the Black Sea at Kilyos and filch a sailor's lantern from the blind ironmonger at Kasimpaşa, five lanterns if necessary

* *dolmuş*: a shared taxi.

and place them all aglow in the night behind the hanging nets, so the birds coming from across the sea will be lured by the lights and fall into the trap. Semih knows well how to set about it. It's not as though he's never eaten one of those nice juicy quails. So has Süleyman. . . Well, fuck it, he's eaten one quail in his life only. Oh fuck it, would Semih refuse Süleyman one wing of the quail he was devouring? Liar! Is there another one as generous as Semih in all of Istanbul? Why, Semih would give his life for a friend, not just a quail's wing, a meagre little bit of meat. . . As for Hayri, he's fed on quails all his life, back there in Rize, his hometown on the Black Sea. Aaah, if only that fool of a father of his, that drunkard, had not shot his next-door neighbour in a moment of rage, that neighbour who had always been like a brother to him. . . Would Hayri's mother ever have sold the family's tea garden then? Never, not if they killed her. Yet she had to, in order to save her husband. All the money went to the lawyers. And after the tea garden. . . They had owned five cows, she sold them too. Then the house went, the huge house where they lived in Rize, and then the large fishing boat on which eight deck hands were employed. Everything the family had was sold and the money handed over to the lawyers who said they needed it to mollify the judges. All that money the judge pocketed, and in the end they sentenced Hayri's father to fifteen years in prison. He'll be released at the next amnesty, for sure, but God knows when that'll be.

Hayri ran away. He left his mother back there in Rize, all alone, penniless, homeless. . . What else could he do?

This is how it came about. One dark wet night, they

70

had fastened their net between the trees and were waiting with their hawks ready for the quails to come... Oh yes, Hayri has caught ever so many quails, he fed on them one time... The quail smells of the sea, of seaweed and of rain. It smells also of wet tree bark. You broil it and, as you eat, the good juicy fat trickles down your chin and fingers. The very thought of it... Well, anyway, they were lying in wait there for the rain of quails, when Hayri moved a little way off from his friends, towards another tree where it was very dark. Why did he go there? He does not remember now. Had somebody called to him, had he heard a sound? He doesn't know. What he remembers is that the minute he reached the tree two strong hands closed over his mouth, so hard he could not breathe, and at the same time another pair of hands gripped his throat. Then he fainted. That's all he remembers. When he opened his eyes again he was in the house of Skipper Temel, another neighbour. Later he learned that it was the two brothers of the neighbour his father had killed who had tried to strangle him. And after that they began to follow Hayri like his shadow. One day, one early dawn maybe, Hayri never says exactly when, he managed to give them the slip. Straightaway he hopped into a fishing vessel heading for Istanbul and thus made good his escape.

Ever since, Hayri has been adrift in Istanbul. That's quite a long time now and there's nothing he hasn't tried his hand at, including all kinds of petty thievery. Yes, Hayri tried, he survived, but there was no future in any of those things. Then one day, when an old man in Fatih, Sado Efendi the cobbler, was reminiscing about his past, as he always did to whoever would listen, young or old, man or woman, deaf or dumb, all the twenty-four hours of the day, non-stop... Well, one day when the boys were listening to him, Sado Efendi told of how he used to trap birds on Florya Plain, how he would sell them in front of mosques and churches and synagogues for "fly and be free", making bags and bags of money, how he then invested the money in this and that business and how he became immensely rich, only to dissipate his fortune in drink and gambling, how through his own foolishness he had come to this... On and on he rambled, making the boys' mouths water. That was the day they stole Aunt Zare's kilim and bought a tent. As for the net, they filched it from a fisherman. What was left of the money they just spent. There's no end to the things you can spend money on in Istanbul. They went to the movies, they bought sunflower seeds, ate ice creams, drank cereal cider, and even took a boat trip to Kadiköy. And they also shot lewd remarks at girls in platform shoes. And why shouldn't they? This is a free country, isn't it? It's nobody's business if they chat up girls, and even go a step further, damn it. Like Semih... He's a smart one, he is... Last year, when he was still only so high, he laid Şero's daughter, Mimi, and even blood came. Everyone heard of it. Semih had to make himself scarce, and for six months he could not set foot in the neighbourhood. Just let Semih get started, he'll go on for ever describing how it happened, down to the smallest detail.

And then, after they've caught all those quails in Kilyos and sold them at the Flower Market, when they've made a good pile, ah then... They'll go straight to that kilim merchant from Antep. No, no, he's not at all a bad fellow, that kilim merchant. At first, he even refused to buy the kilim from the boys. This is a very beautiful kilim, he said. The boys begged and pleaded so hard that the merchant relented. He took the kilim and gave them a small sum of money. Listen, my young lions, he said to them, I'm not going to sell this kilim. As soon as you can find money to repay me, I'll give it back to you. But if you can't, well then, you'll come to me and I'll pay you the rest of what it's worth... And a fortnight later, without even consulting Süleyman, Semih went to the merchant and drew the rest of the money. Süleyman was very annoyed, but he tried not to show it. Such things shouldn't be done, but when it's a friend, and he does it, well it's done. Semih has done a great many things that aren't at all honest... Does a fellow ever run off with a bird that's already been paid for? How can he do that to someone who's been so kind to him? All right, one should be smart to survive, but isn't this going a bit too far? Why, if Ali Şah learns of what Semih has done, he'll send him packing. Semih will never be able to set foot there again. For Ali Şah is the grand *sachem* of the Dolapdere underworld. Would all the roughnecks of Dolapdere be so devoted to him if he wasn't? And who else but him would dare to saunter up and down Beyoğlu in broad daylight with two revolvers stuck in his red sash? No, Semih will never tell Ali Şah what he's done, and then, please God, Ali Şah won't send him packing, he'll train the falcon...

Hayri worries himself sick, thinking of his mother, back there in Rize. He cannot sleep, he cannot rest, so much so that he once bought dope from a fellow in Sirkeci and smoked it. He not only used the dope

73

himself, he sold some to tourists. He didn't like it, though, not Hayri, and he never touched it again, nor did he sell any more of the filthy stuff to tourists.

Besides, Hayri's real name is not Hayri at all. He uses this name so his enemies from Rize will not be able to trace him. You could kill him but he'd never reveal his real name to anyone.

So there you are, if they had enough money, if they could sell all those little birds they catch on Florya Plain, then Süleyman would take the money and he and Semih would travel to Rize and bring Hayri's mother back with them to Istanbul. Somehow, by hook or by crook, Hayri would manage to make her live in comfort. Never, for one moment, is the image of his mother absent from his eyes, and if he is secretive, taciturn, always downcast and melancholy, it is because his mother is all alone there, destitute... There are nights when Hayri, in his sleep, cries out, Mother, Mother, and gives such a sob as to tear his lungs.

In truth, Hayri could long ago have found the money to bring his mother over, but he does not want to become like Semih. Why, if he set himself to it, Hayri could strip the whole of Beyoğlu bare in one day! Suppose he were to pull off a big job, suppose he were to make a sizeable haul, and then sent Süleyman and Semih to Rize to fetch his mother... And they brought her back with them... In the meantime, Hayri has rented one of those small wooden houses in Samatya. Samatya is Hayri's favourite part of the town. He says it reminds him of Rize. And Hayri's mother has moved in, ever so happy at last, and just as she has lifted her hands in a prayer of thanksgiving to God for having

74

blessed her with such a good son, suddenly there is a knock on the door and a whole pack of policemen burst into the house, shouting, where's that thief Hayri? Hayri the thief... His mother, of course, protests. There's no thief in this house, no one by the name of Hayri either. But the police have already spotted him. Here he is, they say, this is the thief we're looking for. And so they clap a pair of jingling handcuffs onto his wrists. It'll be the death blow for Hayri's mother. She'll die of grief on the spot... No, Hayri's not mad. He'll never do anything like that, he'll never become a thief, a criminal. If he did once smoke hashish, it was to relieve the anguish he felt for his mother, and if he left off it was because he thought of her worse than ever when he smoked, because the hashish made him ache with longing for her still more.

Please God, make Ali Şah train the falcon...

Please God, don't let the merchant sell that kilim...

Please God, oh please, please, don't let anything bad happen to Hayri's mother, don't let her enemies hurt her ... Please God, let Süleyman and Semih find her safe and sound in Rize town and bring her with them to Istanbul...

Young girls have such small breasts... Then how do they grow? Ah well, it's the boys make them grow. They caress and fondle them, and those little breasts grow and grow and become like large downy quinces, sweet-smelling, driving the boys crazy. Young as he is, Semih has already made a lot of young girls' breasts grow. Ah yes, Semih has a way with girls. They can't resist him. Why does Semih darken his budding moustache every morning with a pencil? It's so the girls won't protest when he fondles their breasts. Girls

75

adore moustaches, so is it Semih's fault if they fall for him? Hayri, now... He never fools around with girls. Not that he's not fond of them, he even strokes their breasts sometimes, but his heart's not in it. It's his mother he's always thinking of, day in day out. What does he care what Semih does to the girls' breasts! As for Long Süleyman, is it because he's so tall, a real beanpole, or for some other reason that he's ashamed even to look at a girl. Never mind, he'll soon get over it, his turn will come! Aaah, if only one could sport a moustache like Ali Şah's, an Albanian moustache, bushy as a fox's tail... Maybe Süleyman will grow out of it, he won't be so bashful when he's older. Then, maybe the girl Mido... She's smallish, that Mido, but already her breasts are like a grown woman's, and so are her hips, she's had so many boys caressing them... Maybe one day Mido will entice Süleyman to come with her to one of the empty rooms in Zülfikar Pasha's crumbling forty-room old mansion, for Mido has proclaimed it high and low that she is resolved to make love in all of the forty rooms of the mansion, and each time with a different boy. She's her own man, that Mido. When she likes a boy, she leads him on freely. She goes with a whole lot of boys, but with Semih she always remains aloof. She turns her nose up at him when they meet... Just let Semih catch all those quails at Kilyos, large fat quails, smelling of the sea, the brine, the rain... See how he'll sell them, and with the money...

Well, with the money Semih will buy a street peddler's cart. Semih is ever so quick on his feet. Say the police are after him. Why, then he can run like a greyhound. That's God's truth, and no fear that the cops from the Municipality will catch up with him, not even if they're in a car, not even if they've got that superintendent, Death-head Nihat, to lead them. That's what they call him, Death-head Nihat, and he's the sworn enemy of all the vagrant boys in Istanbul. . . Semih will load his peddler's cart with combs, knives, torches, razor blades, sunglasses, and many many other articles, things that sell fast. He won't spend the money on himself at all, not even on food. . . Well, you can't go without food, but even if he's got banks full of money, he'll eat only bread, and bread that he'll steal from the baker's at that. . . It's easy to steal. If he's caught at it, Semih will give the baker a good dressing-down as he has done many a time. . . So what, man, are we to die of hunger when there's so much bread in the world, smelling so good, brown and fresh from the oven? And the baker will feel so guilty that he'll let him go scot-free. There was even that baker who, after having caught Semih stealing his bread, was almost moved to tears by the piteous story Semih told him. So he gave him three large loaves and made him swear that he'd come to bakery whenever he was hungry. Each day, Semih went to that same baker to get a loaf of bread and then sold it to someone or other as soon as he turned the corner, and when he'd saved enough money, the three of them would go straight to the cinema. But some old sneak spotted them and went and blabbed to the baker and the next morning, when Semih arrived for his loaf, the baker pounced on him in such a rage he nearly killed him. Anyone else would have been done for, but Semih somehow managed to shake the man off. He ran for his life, never stopping until he reached the Old Walls by the sea. It took a month for the purple mark on his neck to disappear, the baker had squeezed so hard. Eh, after that, Semih never again. . .

With the money saved from peddling, Semih will first set up shop on the Oil Market wharf. All three of them will work there. Semih knows exactly what each of them will do. All the money the shop brings in they'll save, or almost all of it. They'll put it into banks, and there'll be so much that when Semih enters a bank the manager will rise to his feet to greet him. Then, when they have saved a really big sum, Semih will buy two new shops, one in Eminönü and the other in Beyoğlu, and he'll put Süleyman to manage the one and Hayri the other. Of course, there'll be salesgirls employed in the shops. By that time, Süleyman won't be so shy of girls, so ashamed of his long neck stretching like the neck of a goose and of his bulging eyes that stick out like two fists. And Hayri. . . Oh, he likes girls all right, what man doesn't, but it's because of his mother's warning. . . Don't ever even look at a girl, she had cautioned him, they only get a fellow into trouble. . . And even here, in Istanbul, he keeps to his mother's advice, although now and then he steals a covert look at girls' breasts and at their round bouncing hips, becoming so fascinated he can't take his eyes off them any more. . . When Semih has made still more money from the shops and filled whole banks, he'll set up a factory. What kind of factory? That's something Semih won't tell anyone, not even himself, but it'll be such a factory that Semih will be able to buy three houses on the shores of the Bosphorus. . . He'll put one of his wives in one of the houses, his other wife in another. . . Each of the houses will have such a huge garden that if a boy wanted to hide in it, the police could search a whole month and still not find him. And in the Bay of Bebek, Semih will have boats at anchor, of the kind they call yachts... As for the third house, the largest, well, he'll give it to his dear friends, his brothers, his partners, Hayri and Süleyman...

If ever Semih tries a mean trick on them again, then there'll be hell to pay. Süleyman will plug a bullet right through the centre of his forehead. His tongue will hang out, he'll be covered with blood... And the girl Mido? All this while she'll be bursting with envy, because though Hayri and Süleyman both like her, Semih has made it a condition that not one of them will let her into his house, that little tart. No, no, this won't do, what right has Semih to interfere in everyone's affairs? Do the others meddle with him when he takes girls to the empty houses of pashas, and even when he gets his friends into all kinds of trouble? No, Mido is none of Semih's business. Neither Süleyman nor Hayri would accept such a condition.

Aaah, Ali Şah, come on now, Ali Şah...

And maybe Uncle Mahmut will find a way to sell those cages full of birds, he'll help us get rid of them. And then... Whoopee!

10

〜

"Look here, man," Mahmut said, "they're a funny lot, those young fowlers of yours!"

"Yes," I agreed. "Have you been able to do something for them?"

"I'm trying," he said. "Wait a little. You never know. This town's full of people, so many, swarming like ants... But those people..."

Those people absorbed in themselves, who cannot even see the tip of their own nose... Withdrawn, cowering in their own darkness... Are those the ones to see these bright tiny birds fluttering in cramped cages, waiting to be set free, longing to fly away, even over the polluted waters of the Bosphorus?

"Come now, Mahmut, don't get angry."

But he does get angry, Mahmut, he gets storming mad.

It is not with those who catch the birds and cram them into cages that Mahmut is angry, it is with those who refuse to free them, who refuse to do a good turn, those are the ones he blames.

Tomorrow or the day after, Mahmut will not go fishing as usual. Instead, he will take the boys with their cages full of birds to the courtyard of Sultan Ahmet Mosque, and to the plaza in front of Haghia Sophia, and also to the old Moslem quarter of Üsküdar, and to

Eyup Mosque, and perhaps also to Taksim Square, and even up to the posh quarter of Şişli. He will go in quest of people with still a spark of love for birds, for their fellow human beings. And he will find them, oh he will, he will. Maybe it will be some old woman, a relic of bygone days, wrapped in a white shawl, stepping softly over the earth, light as a fairy, ready to float away... A grandmother who'll hand over two and a half liras and ask for a bird... She'll cradle the bird in her hands and stroke its back with her forefinger, she'll look into the timorous, panic-stricken black eyes and her heart will be filled with a magic love, a deep compassion, and from her thin lips will flow some old forgotten childhood prayer, and her warm breath will caress the bird. Her eyes never leaving it, she will lift her right hand into the air and loosen her grip. The little bird will hesitate at first, it will linger another moment in the warmth of her palm, then it will shoot up, arrow-like, in a joyful sheering flight and vanish between the minarets.

Long years ago, when Mahmut used to go selling birds for "fly and be free", people would come in droves to cast the birds into the air and the whole world would be suffused with joy and love, with the warmth of human beings and of birds. The sky would be overspread with birds, resounding with their cries like a song of gladness. Mahmut always avoided selling his birds to children, for they did not buy them to set them free. Usually, they would tie a string to the bird's feet and play with it, or they would imprison it in a cage that was much too narrow, or even thrust the bird under their shirt where it would stifle to death. Many would be sincerely grieved to have caused the bird's death while they had been playing, forgetting all about it. Others would not be affected at all, or would pretend not to be; they would throw away the dead bird with indifference, as though it were only a stone. Mahmut could recognise both sorts at a glance, from their eyes perhaps, or the way they gestured with their hands, how I don't quite know. A boy who had been distressed at the death of his bird would come and buy another one, which he would then cradle in the palms of his hands, lovingly, cautiously, as though terrified at the idea of hurting it in any way. The other kind would stand apart, glaring angrily at Mahmut and at the birds in their cages.

Well, now, at his age, tomorrow or the day after, Mahmut is going to sell birds again in Istanbul town, he will look for men of good will, still able to feel pity and love. And he will find them. There will always be men of good will, Mahmut claims. He will see if charity and compassion are dead or not. He will cast Istanbul's fortune.

In his youth, a long time ago, Mahmut had sold as many as six hundred birds in a few hours and this in front of only one single mosque, the Valide Sultan, and he had watched them soar into the sky, drowning Eminönü Square and indeed the whole city in a glow of joy and love. The happiness of freeing a bird, of saving a living creature... Mahmut can never forget the childish pleasure, the bliss, the beauty on the faces of those who had just let loose a bird and, their hands empty now, followed it as it winged away until it had quite vanished from sight. He had seen old men, their backs bent with age, clap their hands and even skip with joy like children as the birds flew out of their

82

hands. And shout with laughter too, jubilant, unrestrained. But, today, where is the man in this town who can still laugh like that, with all his heart, at the sight of something that brings beauty, and goodness, and cheer?

"Stop Mahmut, you're talking like them now. . ."

Well, all right, there are some people still like that, of course there are, it's impossible they should all have disappeared. In all this large humanity. . . The human being is made of layer upon layer, and the best of him, the most precious gem, is there, in the innermost layer. As you strip the layers off, one by one, he becomes purer, lovelier. . . What is ugly is mankind's outer shell. A man worthy of the name will always be trying to cast off his own shells and also the shells of all humankind. And as they come off, the world grows brighter. Brighter and brighter. . .

"Stop, Mahmut, stop."

"I won't stop," he shouted. "I won't hear a word against the human race. Never! Somewhere it's still there, the light, shining. . . I know it. And if we cannot find it, it's because we're not strong enough. If we cannot see that bright light, it's because our eyes are blinded by the darkness inside us."

At the very last moment, when you are convinced that all hope is lost, humanity will suddenly shine forth, and hope will blossom like a flower.

Long before the foundation of Istanbul, already these tiny little birds, coming from who knows where to leave again for a place unknown, would descend in a rain of many colours over the dried thistles of Florya Plain. They would devour the seeds and grow strong, then take wing, driven by the rough December winds,

83

and fly off to another part of the world, to new fields of thistles. But maybe they nested in some far-off thistle-less plain where no bird flies or caravan passes. And on that vast plain the females laid their eggs among tall grasses in the millions of nests they had built, and sat on them, warm and snug, in the supreme bliss of motherhood... And the males carried minute seeds to their brooding mates. And the millions of hatched chicks, tiny, each one no bigger than a beetle, would open their beaks wide and clamour for food. Maybe the plain would be covered with flowers. Maybe the fledglings thrived, not on thistle seeds, but on the delicate seeds of flowers.

Maybe at the time the city was founded all this area where the wood is now, and Yeşilköy, Şenlikköy, Bakirköy, Florya Plain, was just one vast stretch of thistles which the millions of birds born on that far-off plain would overrun in a shower of colour and light. But perhaps they had been born on some thistly mountainside, these birds, or in some forest... Perhaps...

Children, from Oriental Rome onwards, through Byzantium and the Ottoman Empire, would set snares and baits to capture these birds, and ever since that time the birds would be there, waiting to be freed in front of churches, mosques and synagogues. This had become a tradition with the people of the city, and so had the calling of the fowler.

With the passing of years, the thistle fields diminished gradually. New settlements sprang up and expanded, Şenlikköy, Yeşilköy, Ambarli, Cennetmahallesi, Telsizler, Menekşe, Florya, Basinköy. Ugly concrete apartment blocks began to crowd the lovely dale of Florya where violets used to grow. And now only this small tract of land between Menekşe and Basinköy, between the sea and the wood, is left for the birds. Here, there are still some thistle shrubs, and this is where the birds return every year for their beloved thistle seeds. But last year, the owner of the land parcelled it out and sold the plots to new-rich buyers for as much as five hundred liras per square metre. A new gold rush is on in Istanbul, the rush to buy building sites. For a mere span of land, these greedy new-rich monsters will gouge each other's eyes out. They will kill and rape and cut throats. . . For a mere span of land! And next year, in place of this copper-hued thistle field, there will be a mass of concrete, villas, apartment buildings, so ugly that the mere sight of them will be nauseating. And in the new streets, alienated creatures who live only for lucre and ostentation will be strutting about, showing off to each other. They will own motorcars that they will drive at a hundred and fifty, two hundred kilometres an hour along the London Highway to get here, hitting and killing people on the way. . .

And maybe the birds, impelled by some ancient, deep-rooted instinct, will come again to the sky over where that lofty plane tree is now but which will have been cut down by then. They will pause a moment, searching for something, vaguely remembering. They will flutter in little groups over the concrete agglomeration of houses, and finding nowhere to alight will take themselves off like some remote sorrow.

"Don't, Mahmut! Stop, please stop."

"We must cast Istanbul's fortune once more. One last time. . ."

85

11
~~~

That day it rained till nightfall. At one time, the weather seemed to be clearing up and the sea in front of Ambarli was like glazed frost. Then a dark cloud spread over the sky, covering everything, and it started to rain again.

Early next morning, I awoke to a pure and cloudless sky, washed clean and gleaming like blue velvet. A large airliner glided over the Islands and landed at Yeşilköy Airport with a great roar, leaving the sky empty again, as empty as if no plane had ever flown in it up to now, not a bird even, a perfectly silent, very distant, very wide blue sky that would remain undisturbed till the end of time.

Though I was anxious to know how things had turned out with the boys, I hesitated to go to them for fear they might think I was coming about the falcon, or to get back the money. It was days, too, since I'd seen Mahmut.

I started down the slope to Menekşe. On the way, I saw Hüseyin Uzuntaş riding full speed downhill to the train station on the bicycle his father, who worked at a foundry, had made for him with his own hands. Cano was repairing a fish net. Tatar Ali had gone to the Golden Horn to weave nets for some fishermen there. Had he come back? I wondered. Nuri, I knew, had been out fishing the night before. Maybe Mahmut had accompanied him... I looked into the coffee house. Old Hakki was there, playing gin rummy with Haydar Uyanik. The rowing boats and fishing craft were drawn upstream, away from the sea, and lay idle, a medley of many bright colours. Özkan and Ahmet the Jap were busy painting a boat orange. Kazim Aga sat in front of the coffee house, his reddened lashless eyes blinking as he peered at the sunny sky and the glinting sand. There was no one else around.

I went on along the shore towards the Florya beaches. At his Family Casino, Veysel was alone, listening to the radio. A fat man in long white underpants, obviously very cold, his hands thrust between his thighs, was entering the water. I walked on past the presidential summer residence and came to the great plane tree in front of the Municipal Beach. A muffled booming came from the tree, scarcely audible. Its leaves were all yellow now, and turning red. Three bright red leaves came spiralling down very slowly and dropped in front of me. I looked up to see if the topmost leaves of the tree had turned red too, but these were only just becoming yellow. And as I looked I was astounded to see a very large hawk floating up there, right above the plane tree, its pointed wings stretched wide, quite motionless, as though nailed to the sky. But no, no hawk could be as large as that, nor with wings as broad. There were eagles in these parts, medium-sized tawny eagles. Last year, Nevzat had found one with a broken wing in the woods. It was a thing of beauty, that eagle, a marvel of nature. The instant its wing healed, it had flown away. Not another day had it remained in Nevzat's house. Maybe this was a tawny eagle flying up there now. Why, if the boys managed to capture it for me, I'd give them anything they wanted . . .

Now I felt I could safely go to them with that eagle floating in the sky. I passed under the bridge and, hurrying along the path between the wood and the poplar copse, I came to the tent.

The boys greeted me with joy.

Süleyman flung his arms out as though ready to take wing.

"Look, Abi, look!" he cried. "Just look at what's up there! You came and you brought that hawk with you."

"That's not a hawk. Don't you see? It's a tawny eagle," I said.

Süleyman's face fell.

"So it's a tawny eagle," he murmured, all his joy gone, deflated like a pricked balloon.

I laughed. "What's the difference? If you can get that eagle for me, then I'll give you anything you ask."

At that, both of them became gay as larks.

"Why, think!" I said. "A tawny eagle's nothing like a hawk. Hawks only hunt for quail, but eagles, especially tawny eagles like this one, catch rabbits too."

Süleyman's eyes sparkled.

"A rabbit can sell for forty liras, can't it?" he asked quickly.

"Forty liras, yes, even fifty," I said. "It depends on the size of the rabbit."

He gave this a thought, then looked straight into my eyes.

"If we could take this eagle to Ali Şah .." he ventured.

88

"You've got to catch it first," I said.

"That's easy," he said. "See how it's stuck there? See how nungrily it's looking at our decoys, its head bent this way? It won't take long to lure it down. But what a huge bird it is. . . What if it tears the net?"

"I'll get you a new one. Just you catch it."

"I wonder if it's the only tawny eagle around here," Süleyman said artfully.

"No, it can't be the only one," I said.

"Good. Abi, come back this evening and your bird will be ready for you."

"All right," I said.

Discreetly, without his seeing, I slipped some notes into his pocket. Süleyman realised at once what I was doing. He turned and looked at me with love. His large eyes were brimming with tears.

"Tomorrow," he said, "Mahmut Abi will come."

Hayri, roused from his reverie, chipped in. "We're going to take the birds to town to sell them. Look, he's brought us three new cages, each one as big as a room."

He pointed to the cages at the foot of the barbed wire fence. Like the other cages, Mahmut's too were now chock-full of birds, each cage a crammed seething mass of many colours.

As I left, Süleyman, his eyes on the tawny eagle, shouted after me. "Look, Abi, the bird's drawing nearer and nearer. It'll be yours when you come tonight."

"I'll be back," I assured him.

I went home and sat down in front of the window. From there, I could watch the bird and see if it did make a go for the decoys.

Evening came, the sun went down, and still the eagle was there, hovering high above the plane tree, its wings outstretched, never moving, as though nailed to the sky. And so it remained till nightfall, never changing its stance. And then it was too dark to see anything. The poplar, the plane tree and the eagle faded into the night.

How relieved the boys must be that I had not come back as promised, how glad. . .

12

~~

"Confound it," Mahmut cursed, "if only I had a little money. Damn this life. People aren't like human beings any more. Aaah, just a little money. . ."

"They wouldn't take it," I remarked.

He stopped and stared at me.

"You're damn right they wouldn't!" he exclaimed and his eyes brightened as though he had glimpsed a ray of hope, some honour left in the world. "Of course they wouldn't take money just like that."

"Where are they now, Mahmut?" I inquired. "D'you know if they've caught some large bird of prey, an eagle, a hawk, a kite?"

After a moment's reflection, Mahmut shook his head.

"No such thing," he said.

"Where are they now, the boys?"

"Where would they be?" Mahmut laughed. "There, by their tent, trapping birds again. All the time. . . Their eyes fixed on the sky, waiting, hoping against hope for a large tawny eagle to fall into their nets."

I looked up. The bird of prey was there, circling above the plane tree high up in the sky. I could swear its wings quivered with desire and hunger, as though it had caught some delectable scent. Any moment now it would swoop down over the decoys by the clap-net. . .

"I saw it too," Mahmut declared, pleased.

"That's what they're waiting for," I said.

"Yes," he said glumly. "And I have to be off at dawn the day after tomorrow. I'm going fishing down by the Çanakkale Strait. I'll be away for several weeks."

I gave a start.

"But what about the children?" I cried. "And all those cages full of birds?"

"We'll leave that to the grace of God," Mahmut said and smiled.

13

~~~

Clearly, Mahmut had not much faith in churches, mosques and synagogues, nor in the bustling quarter of Sirkeci. They loaded up the cages and started off.

"We'll go to the squatters' neighbourhood of Kazliçeşme first," Mahmut decided. "The people there are newly come from Anatolia. Maybe it'll work with them..."

"Let's go," Süleyman said.

Hayri followed last.

They got off the train at Kazliçeşme station, Mahmut first, then Long Süleyman, carrying the two largest cages, his neck stretching longer and longer as though it would snap off, the cages crammed to suffocation, and last of all again Hayri.

Mahmut led them straightaway to the largest square of Kazliçeşme. There, in front of a fountain of rough-hewn limestone from whose tap a trickle of water, only two fingers thick, was flowing into a large tin can, an olive-complexioned, large-eyed girl, barefooted, her hair braided in the traditional forty plaits, stood waiting for the can to fill. Behind her was a row of more girls, also barefooted, and of women, old and young, wearing flowered calico dresses and gumshoes. In a corner of the square, a group of fifteen or twenty men were crowding over something they seemed to be repairing, a motorcyle perhaps. Further off, three little boys were bowling a hoop.

They set the cages down in the middle of the square and, in a moment, out of nowhere, a crowd had gathered in a circle round them. First, a multitude of children, then some very old people, the women from the fountain, the men who were repairing the motorcycle, and still more and more, the newcomers breaking through the circle to have a look at the cages, wondering what these birds had been brought here for, expectant.

There was a long silence. Then a youth approached Mahmut and ventured to ask a question.

"These birds..." Mahmut began, but suddenly found it difficult to explain what this was all about. "These birds... We've brought them so you can buy them, because..." He stopped, unable to say another word.

"Yes, yes, but why should we buy them? What for?" the youth insisted. He, too, wore gumshoes. They were coated with mud. His patched washed-out trousers stuck tightly to his legs and the sleeves of his cheap purplish brown vest were worn and frayed. He had huge hands and he was now holding them out, palms up, in a gesture of bewilderment.

Before Mahmut could find something to say, an old man with a drooping grey moustache broke in.

"Don't you see?" he said. "What's so surprising about this? These birds are for sale. We buy them to keep in a cage and to listen to their song every morning." He paused a moment. "And in the evening too," he added.

"Shame!" an old woman cried. "These poor little

birds, so beautiful, each one no bigger than a thumb, they've stuffed them one on top of the other in those cages! Look how the poor things can't even move!"

"No, no," Süleyman said hastily. "It's not for putting into cages that we're selling them. As you can see, they couldn't last two days packed like that in those cages. It's to set them free, to save them from dying that you'll buy them."

"What? What did you say?" a young lad piped out mockingly. "What is it we're supposed to do?"

"To buy them and then. . ."

A vigorous pinch in the thigh from Hayri shut Süleyman up.

"Hah-hah-ha," someone guffawed. "So we buy a bird and throw it into the air, eh? Hah-ha. . . Let's hope they're not too dear. How much for a bird?"

"Two and a half liras," Süleyman replied without thinking.

"You mean I'm to give you two and a half liras for a bird that I'll throw away at once, is that it?" a long-faced woman in a tight black headcloth inquired.

"Well, yes," Süleyman said.

"And why should I do that, I'd like to know?"

"Why? For a good deed! To do a good deed so that . . ."

"That's a good one!" a short yellow-haired youth chimed in. "So you go catching birds and, doing so, you commit a sin, and we save them and do a good deed, eh?"

More and more people were pressing around them. Catching sight of the crowd in the square, they hurried up, out of houses and shops to find out what was happening.

"Listen," Süleyman said, raising his voice, "for just two and a half liras you buy one of these little birds, then you say a prayer over it and cast it up into the sky. It will fly off, free. . ."

The onlookers held their breath, waiting for Süleyman to continue. Mahmut and Hayri were bathed in sweat, but Süleyman was made of harder stuff.

"And where will it fly to, you will ask? Straight to Paradise! So that when you die and pass into the other world, that bird will be there, waiting for you at the gates of Paradise. . ."

A shrill woman's voice cut him short.

"Ugh! Perish your mother, you lying little brat. . ."

A ripple of laughter passed through the crowd.

"May your two eyes drop in front of you!" the woman in the black headcloth shrieked.

"They haven't left a bird in the sky, the godless heathens!" a young girl exclaimed. "Pigs, that's what they are!"

"God damn you! Damn you, damn you!" a crystal-line voice kept repeating.

By now the square was filled to overflowing, worse than on a festival day. Each newcomer, after inspecting the cages, joined in the general argument, airing his own views on birds and sin and good deeds.

"It's a sin. . ."

"A good deed. . ."

"But they're so tiny. . ."

"Look how they shine in that cage, like the sun!"

"They won't last long in there. . ."

"Packed tight!"

"The devil take that wretched beanpole! Piling in those birds like you would pile cotton or press

96

cheese. . ."

"May a fast-moving bullet do away with that longshanks!"

"Let's free them!"

"Yes, yes, since it's a good deed. . ."

"Let's open those cages right away."

"No, no, it's a pity for those poor blokes."

"Yes, who knows how many days they spent catching them."

"Maybe it's true that you go to Paradise if you free a bird."

"Oh, go on, you! Paradise, my foot!"

"They're all cheats, these fellows."

"They may be doing this only to earn their daily bread."

"True, look at that long one, just skin and bones, he is."

"It's sinning against these birds got him into that state!"

"Just let him go on capturing birds, that long one. . ."

"Go on, go on, longshanks, and see if God doesn't cast the crippling spell on you. . ."

"Have you no father, no mother?"

"Have they never told you it's a sin to catch birds that are so small?"

"Haven't they told you that you could roast in Hell for this?"

"That in this world, too, your life will be nothing but one long misery?"

"Without respite, ever. . ."

Kazlıçeşme Square was in an uproar. Some wanted to break the cages and free the birds, others to fling Süleyman to the ground and give him a proper thrashing, while still others were taking up his defence. In the middle of the crowd, Mahmut and Hayri stood unnoticed now, while Long Süleyman was the sole focus of attention. His neck longer than ever, bathed in sweat, his eyes bulging, bewildered, he still held his own against the taunting, spitting crowd. At the same time, he tried to answer the well-meaning questions of those who had taken pity on him.

How, by what means did they make good their escape? Was it by some move of Mahmut's or had a friend of his come to their rescue? Perhaps a policeman had intervened and blown his whistle. Even Mahmut never quite realised how they found themselves on the platform of the railway station, free from the mob. They got into a train. Oh, the relief of it! Even from there, the clamour of voices from the square still reached their ears.

They got off at the Sirkeci terminal and, pressing through the throng, put their cages down in front of the Valide Mosque. Straightaway, Süleyman ran up the steps that led to the mosque and began to shout.

"Fly little bird, free as the air, and meet me at the gates of Paradise!"

Here, too, people gathered around the cages, but they only gave the birds a glance and turned away almost at once. Another group formed, then another...

Suddenly, a miracle happened. A young man of about twenty-five stopped in front of the cages, staring at the birds. He was wearing rubber shoes and long embroidered woollen stockings drawn up to the knees over his trousers. His glossy black hair fell over his brow and he had black eyebrows that met above his nose. For a while he stood there, arms akimbo, and his

98

eyes went from the birds to the sky above, as though searching for something, then to the pigeons pecking away at seeds on the paving stones. Sadly, his gaze fell back on the cages and, very slowly, he drew from his pocket a country pouch embroidered in blue.

"How much are these birds?" he asked in a deep strong voice that carried authority.

"Two and a half liras," Süleyman replied quickly.

The man bent down and inspected the cage.

"This one," he said to Süleyman, pointing at a bird. "And this one too. And that one."

Joyfully, Süleyman plunged his hand into the cage and fished out three birds.

The man took them one by one. At the third, he frowned.

"This isn't the one I wanted. You've given me the wrong one. Look, that one." And he pointed to a bird with its wing protruding out of the cage. "That's it, that's it," he cried.

From the meshes of the cage Süleyman extricated a largish bird with a bright red breast. The man had the money ready. He handed over the three banknotes and walked away, breathing a prayer over the birds. Stopping under the arcade of the mosque, he caressed one of the birds, then cast it swiftly into the air. The bird shot up and disappeared above the dome of the mosque. Again, as though throwing a stone, he flung the second bird up, then the third. After that, his head bent, he went past the toy stalls in the archway and, dodging through the traffic, crossed over to the pavement in front of the Iş Bank. There he stopped, thrust his hands into his pockets and began scrutinising the sky over Valide Mosque.

For a while there was a trickle of buyers. One little boy, after hesitating half an hour, at last made his choice and, holding the bird close to his breast, ran off, slipping through the cars and on to the Galata Bridge.

But soon the number of buyers dwindled to nothing. Still they waited, hope rising with every passer-by who paused to look at the cages, then falling again when the person moved on without buying a single bird.

Süleyman was hoarse with shouting.

"Fly little bird, free as the air, and meet me at the gates of Paradise."

Meet me there, damn it, damn it, meet me at the gates of Paradise. . .

His voice was lost among the honking of cars and the shrill cries of hawkers who had displayed their wares in front of the mosque, razor blades, combs, plastic flowers, knives, screws, black-market cigarettes, brooms, old books and magazines, sunflower seeds. . .

After this, Riza, a friend of Mahmut's who drove a taxi, took them first to the Süleymaniye Mosque, then to the Eyup Mosque, without charging them anything. In front of Süleymaniye Mosque, things almost took a drastic turn. But for Mahmut, one of those round-bearded, bereted zealots, a huge man, would have smashed the cages, killed the birds and torn the boys piecemeal. He was coming out of the mosque telling the beads of his *tesbih** when he spotted the boys with their birds and charged at them like an angry bull. But Mahmut moved more swiftly. He flung himself between the zealot and the boys, who grabbed the cages and made a dash for Riza's taxi, running for their

* *tesbih*: prayer beads.

lives. Mahmut soon joined them and they quickly drove off.

The courtyard of Eyup Mosque was quite deserted. There were the usual pigeons and a lone stork pacing up and down and also, crouching in a corner, a young boy wearing a skullcap and reading the Koran. And not another soul in sight. . .

As a last kindness, Riza drove them all the way up to Taksim. There he left them and went back to Menekşe.

Taksim Square was teeming with crowds of people. Six pigeons had perched on the Monument of the Republic. The Continental Hotel loomed high above the square, like a large four-cornered minaret.

They dragged their cages to the steps that led into the park. The place where they had stopped smelled strongly of urine. Hayri looked around to see whether there was a stable or something nearby. Then he realised that the stink came from the wall beside the steps.

Traffic lights kept blinking, green, red, yellow. Cars and people surged through the place, all in a tangle, and the blast of automobile horns mingled with the voices of the crowds in a deafening roar. Meatball vendors, newsboys, gypsy flower-sellers with their baskets lined along the pavement, shoeblacks in a long row, their boxes gleaming like gold, taxi station barkers shouting at the tops of their voices, men and women pressing and pushing, scuttling this way and that to escape being run down by the cars, a barefooted villager rubbing shoulders with a fur-clad woman, elegant florist shops, dirty pavements littered with paper and vomit, petrol fumes mingling with the stink

101

of urine... All in a rolling snarl...

Hayri had crouched down in a corner of the steps, his head drawn between his shoulders.

"What a lot of people!" he said.

Mahmut smiled at him.

"Yes," he said. "And not one laughing face..."

It was with new eyes that he was gazing at the crowds.

Süleyman stood by, his eyes bulging, his neck longer than ever. He was so shaken by the noise and confusion that his mind had gone blank. Forgotten were the birds, Hayri, Mahmut, even his own self. It was a dreamworld of teeming humanity he was floating in, of huge apartment blocks and rushing traffic. The odour of greasy smoke drifting from the meatball barbecue carts made him come to himself. It was an odour that could drive a man crazy with hunger. His eyes focused on the meatball vendors. The nearest cart was set on small wheels. It was painted blue, with a design of tiny pink flowers and pale green leaves. A glass-paned showcase was set on the cart, and, beside it, a brazier piled with glowing embers. It was a beautiful copper brazier, and from it rose a tall stovepipe, maybe two metres high. In the showcase were meatballs, ready to be grilled, a mound of minced meat in reserve, bright red tomatoes, parsley and onions. And right in the middle was a large rose, a pink full-blown Ottoman rose. The meatball merchant had a drooping light brown moustache. His knee breeches were bound at the waist with a wide black sash. He was counting some money. Süleyman stared. What long fingers he had! Instinctively, he glanced at his own hands, then his eyes returned to the man, examining him from top to toe, and came to rest on the long, blunt face which had the sad resentful expression of someone struggling to overcome his lack of faith in himself and in life.

Mahmut was gazing at the birds, agonising in their cages, at the boys, the pressing crowds, the traffic. He was remembering. . .

He had spent exactly three and a half years of his life polishing shoes in Taksim Square. His place had been right there, the sixth in the row of shoeshiners. His box, inlaid with nacre in the shape of fish, trees, clouds and even a mermaid, had been famous, not only among his fellow shoeshiners, but in the whole of Istanbul too. It was the last box that Mestan, the master craftsman at Bakirköy, had made before his death. And what's more, Master Mestan, who never learned to read or write, who in all his life had never put his signature on a piece of paper, but always marked documents with his thumb, well, on this shoeshine box, he had engraved his sign on a blue inlay of nacre. It looked like a character from a cuneiform or Chinese script, a hieroglyph, a bird in flight, but more than anything it looked like Master Mestan himself. Mahmut could swear that Mestan's signature on the box was the very likeness of the master, as though it had been taken at the studio of Foto-Sabah! How could an inscription, and such an elaborate one at that, ever resemble a human face? Mahmut could not explain this, but so it was. Besides, there were those words Master Mestan had spoken when he'd given him the box. "Here," he had said, "take your box, Mahmut, my son, I've fashioned many shoeshine boxes in my life, but in never a single one have I put Mestan. . . Take it and may it bring you luck."

How he had laughed then, showing his toothless gums. . . It warmed Mahmut's heart to think of the old craftsman, here, beside the two children with their cages of half-dead birds, in the midst of the doomsday confusion of the square. His mind went back to the day Master Mestan had given him the shoeshine box. How he had flown at once to Taksim Square. . . He remembered his first client. The man had been struck dumb by Mahmut's joy which communicated itself to every living thing, to the whole world, to the very earth and stones and passing cars. He must have felt it in the marrow of his bones, for instead of paying Mahmut when he had finished, he just stood there, the money passing from one hand to the other, and then, suddenly, he had turned away, his legs dancing, flying, and had vanished in the crowd. Here, today, if the boys could manage to sell some birds, with what joy would they go back to Menekşe, their feet hardly touching the ground, just like Mahmut on that day long ago. . . Süleyman was still gaping, entranced at the meatball merchant. Let him look on, Mahmut thought, better let him be until. . .

Make it twenty, Süleyman heard a man say. The meatball seller kept wiping his hands on the blue apron he wore. He was short and thin, young too, twenty-five maybe. On his right cheek was a deep scar, the result of an Aleppo boil. His eyes were large and of the clearest blue, and even at that distance Süleyman could see how they shone.

Mahmut, and Hayri too from where he was crouching, were watching the meatball man as with deft hands he quickly disposed the meatballs on the greasy blackened grill over the embers. When they were done, he sliced open a half-loaf of bread and with a small pair of tongs picked up the meatballs one by one, very carefully so as not to damage them, and inserted them into the loaf. He added a sprinkling of parsley, a little chopped onion and a couple of tomato slices. Then, wrapping the bread in a pink sheet of paper, he handed it over to his customer. Smoke was still swirling from the stovepipe, spreading that aroma, maddening for empty stomachs.

The customer, darting anxious glances to right and left, hastily bit into the bread. Such a large mouthful it was that his cheeks swelled. With another quick look around, he hurried away, still munching very fast, and disappeared into the crowd. The meatball man followed him with smiling eyes.

Mahmut, too, was smiling, maybe at the boys, maybe at something else... He was trying to decipher some words that had been scrawled in a clumsy hand on the side of the cart. And when he did, it made him so happy that for a moment he forgot the heavy pain weighing deep down inside him at the plight of these boys and of the birds dying in their cages. Stumbling over the syllables, he read it out aloud: Look not for fire in Hell, each man brings his own fire... Yes, Mahmut murmured, from this earth each takes his fire...

There were inscriptions like this one on every barbecue cart that was spitting greasy fumes about the crowded square. One said: Never say die, Erzurum town, bring thou solace to my soul... Another: Bread and sweat, toil and trouble, so goes this bastard world... And still another: Roads, days, life, all things must end, but Istanbul town never will end... This one had been traced on a blue background with tiny flowers painted between the letters.

Suddenly, a loud tumult broke out and people began shouting and rushing about. Meatball vendors hastily gathered up their tongs and knives and pushed off at a running pace, scattering bread and tomatoes on the pavement. The shoeblacks clapped their boxes onto their backs and bolted. All the itinerant vendors were running for their lives. A taxi driver emerged from his car and started hurling oaths at all and sundry, cursing his own luck too in ringing tones that rose above the hubbub. The crowds of pedestrians had stopped to watch. Hayri was on his feet, aghast, ready to take flight, while Süleyman, his eyes wide with fear, bulging more than ever, stood craning his neck as though about to dive from the steps into the square.

Mahmut too was seized with alarm.

"Come," he cried. "Hurry! Take the cages, quick. . ."

Without waiting, he grabbed a couple of cages and made a dash for Taksim Park. Süleyman and Hayri sprinted after him carrying the other cages in which the flurried birds were twittering shrilly. They put the cages down behind the pedestal of the İnönü Monument. Just then, men in green uniforms erupted into the now almost deserted square and charged angrily at whatever came their way. Then, after a while, their rage spent, they reassembled and, all in a group, took themselves off.

The instant they had gone, the meatball carts, the shoeshine boxes, the stalls of itinerant vendors appeared again, and in greater number than before. Where a little while ago there had been not a single

106

vendor of *helva* wafers, now three of them had materialised and were airily trundling their white-painted carts. One of them was calling out at the top of his voice: "Good honeyed *helva*! Honey, pure honey!" He was shouting so hard that it brought tears to his eyes. The whole place rang with his vibrant cries.

"Those were police," Mahmut explained. "Municipality police. . . Quick, back to the steps. The field's clear now. Just right. . ."

They toted the cages back and set them down on the steps again.

Mahmut decided he would do the calling first.

"Fly and be free, fly little bird. . . Free. . ."

He modulated his voice into a warm moving song and suddenly there was quite a crowd forming around them.

"Fly little bird, free as the air, and meet me at the gates of Paradise! Paradise, ah Paradise. . ."

Mahmut had made it into a real song now. It was for these boys. Not for the world, not if they killed him would he have done such a thing, not in his wildest dreams. Yet here he was, he, Mahmut, hawking birds in crowded Taksim Square, and singing too, as though it was a lullaby or a hymn. The idea that he was doing this only for the boys gave him a noble feeling. He had even begun to like the sound of his own voice.

The crowd kept growing. Soon people were crushing each other to get a glimpse of the birds. Completely carried away now, Mahmut drifted from mode to mode, and it must have been half an hour or more before he was aware that no one had yet bought a single bird!

He blew his top.

"Well, why don't you buy one, damn it? These birds are for sale. If you don't buy them for 'fly and be free', they'll all die in their cages, damn it. . ."

There was not the slightest reaction from the onlookers. They just stood and stared at the exhausted birds which were struggling and twittering more feebly now in their cages. Their eyes, too, were slowly losing their brightness.

"Come on, my friends," Mahmut entreated, "buy a bird, it costs so little, nothing really. Look, these boys here, instead of turning to sharp practices, instead of cheating and thieving and picking pockets, these boys are giving you the chance to do a good deed. Think, a good deed! It's for this that they've captured all these birds. Come on, brothers, buy them! Buy these birds and cast them up, free, into the sky. Watch them fly away, full of joy. . . Come on, brothers. . ."

He gazed at the sky. A white cloud floated right above, a round, perfectly white cloud. Mahmut smiled. His eyes, full of hope now, rested on the crowd again and he went on, his voice growing more and more impassioned.

"My friends, my compassionate brothers, what human being, what heart could remain unmoved and allow these birds to die in their cages? No one, no one! Buy them, my brothers, buy them and set them free. Free them so they can fly for your own good, to wait for you at the gates of beautiful Paradise. . ."

Standing there, on the fifth step, above the crowd, he was like a prophet exhorting his fellow men to pity and compassion for all God's creatures, for the birds and beasts and insects. . . His voice rose and fell, now full of wrath, now gentle, appealing, a moaning plaint.

"Look, brothers, look at these birds, at these children here, just kids. . ."

He waved his hand at the boys.

"It's because they had faith, faith in you, that they caught all those birds. If they hadn't trusted you, would they ever have caught so many and been the cause of their death? These kids are human beings too, aren't they? They've got human feelings too, haven't they? If they hadn't, instead of messing about with birds, they could well have become thieves. Or even murderers. . ."

Suddenly he lost his temper. Such was his rage that he jabbered on incoherently, while the onlookers, forgetting the birds, stared at him in amazement.

"Murderers! And kill you instead of these birds! Kill. . ."

With difficulty, he controlled himself and went on more calmly.

"It's because they trusted you, these kids. . . Because that's how it's been for centuries, the children catch these little birds and men of good will, with pity in their hearts, buy them and cast them up, high up. . ."

He pointed at the sky. The white cloud was still there, glowing in a flood of light.

"Buy them, brothers, buy these birds! Come on, they don't cost much, only the price of a *simit*,* ten liras. No, no, five liras." This still seemed too much to Mahmut. He lowered the price again. "And some you can have for two and a half liras. Only two and a half!"

His voice was growing hoarse.

"Well, what are you waiting for, my friends?" he said. "Look what a lovely day it is, and the sun shining

* *simit*: a ring-shaped special kind of bread.

so brightly... Isn't it a shame to see these poor little birds cooped up like this in a cage on such a lovely day? Now, tell me, isn't it?"

He had lapsed into a faint mumble, as though talking to himself, and the crowd, losing interest, was beginning to break up. Seeing the people turning away after all the trouble he'd had getting them together, Mahmut exerted himself afresh.

"This way, brothers, this way! Free a bird and win a place in Paradise. Like this..."

Running to the cages, he extracted a largish bird and took up his stand on the steps again. With the bird cradled in his hands, he made as if he were praying over it, then, lifting his right hand as high as he could, he opened his fingers. The bird darted away at once. It flew first over the Opera building, turned to the Continental Hotel, veered off over Taksim Park and the Sheraton and vanished in the direction of the Bosphorus.

Mahmut rushed back to the cages. One after the other, he took the birds and cast them up into the air.

"Like this, like this!" he shouted.

It was no use. The crowd kept drifting away.

"Like this! So, so!" Frantically he flung one last bird into the air as though casting a stone. Exhausted, his brow and hair wet with perspiration, he glared at the last stragglers.

"Shame on you! Damn you all, you godforsaken creatures... Shame!"

People stared at him, astonished, as he collapsed on the lowest step, his head hanging.

It was some time before he could bring himself to look at the boys. There was no one left by the cages now. The two boys were all alone, Süleyman, his neck still stretched to snapping point, Hayri huddled in a corner. Mahmut longed to get away from it all, but how could he leave the boys among these brutes when he had brought them here himself?

It was then that another miracle happened. An old gentleman with white hair was passing by, leaning on his cane. He stopped near the cages, smiling, and then, as though some distant memory was stirring in him, he turned to Süleyman.

"So it's birds you've got there, is it?" he asked gently.

"Birds. . . Yes . ." Süleyman faltered.

"So! Birds. . . In my young days, boys like you always sold birds like this, come autumn time. I used to myself. . . How much are these birds?"

"Give me whatever you like," Süleyman said in a surly gruff voice, ashamed to show his joy.

In the same instant he regretted having answered so roughly, but the old gentleman held out three five-lira notes.

"Give me three," he said.

"Certainly, right away, good uncle. . ."

Quickly, with trembling hands, Süleyman took out three birds and put them into the hands of this unexpected customer. His cane hanging from his arm, the old gentleman lifted his head towards the white cloud. Very gently, he let go of the birds and, after one last look, shuffled on, still with that happy smile on his lips.

Süleyman dashed down the steps to Mahmut. His face was flushed with joy.

"Look," he said, showing him the fifteen liras.

"Good. Put that in your pocket," Mahmut told him.

"Come with me now," Süleyman said.

"You're doing very well by yourself," Mahmut said. He took a cigarette from his pocket, lit it and inhaled deeply. "Go on now," he insisted, wiping the sweat from his brow. "I'll be right here, waiting."

Süleyman ran back to the cages. Ah, he thought as he stood on the steps gazing at the crowds, so many, many people, if they only bought one bird each and set it free, not forgetting to say a prayer, how lovely it would be, how lovely... His eyes kept going to a meatball cart nearby. It was painted blue and all around the edge was a design of pink flowers with orange eyes, magic flowers, not to be found on this earth. In the centre, under a cluster of white clouds, was a lake, blue-green, radiantly bright, with swans swimming on it, exactly seven swans, long-necked, majestic, and on the shore of the lake was a slender clump of reeds and little mauve and red flowers that were also not of this world. Cranes in bevelled formation flew from one end of the cart to the other. On the opposite side of the cart, a running deer had been painted, dream-like, enchanted, and above it a copper eagle with broad wings and wild razor-sharp eyes. The wheels on which the cart was set were old bicycle wheels, but their nickel plating was polished bright. The brazier on the cart was alight and blue flames rose from the live coals. The meatball vendor, a young man of medium height with large hazel eyes and a trim pointed moustache, wore a blue apron on which a young girl, his betrothed no doubt, had painstakingly embroidered a rose, large and bright yellow. He was a brisk breezy fellow who could not keep still one minute, always on

112

the go, now wiping his tomatoes with a paper handker-
chief to make them shine, next piling up green pep-
pers, then, dissatisfied, aligning them neatly side by
side. A wide grin on his face, he kept chaffing the other
meatball vendors and the shoeshine boys next to him
and cheerfully bandying words with anyone who came
his way.

By now, the square was covered with orange rinds,
torn paper, empty plastic bags, cucumber peelings,
cabbage leaves and all kinds of rubbish.

Suddenly, Süleyman was roused from his reverie.

"Hey, boy," a young man was addressing him, "are
these birds yours?"

Süleyman jumped as though startled out of sleep.

"They're mine," he mumbled.

"How much?"

"Ten liras," Süleyman said boldly.

"Indeed?"

The young man crouched in front of the cages and
stared fixedly. Then, he opened the door of the largest
cage and began taking out birds. One by one, he thrust
them into his shirt.

"Five," he said, straightening up, and he handed
Süleyman a fifty-lira note. Without stopping he made
straight off in the direction of the Bayonet Monument,
trampling over the green lawn, and disappeared down
Kazanci slope.

Süleyman, mesmerised, was still gaping at the fifty-
lira note when Hayri called out to him.

"Put that money away, will you!"

Süleyman burst out laughing. He shoved the money
into his pocket, but he could not stop himself, he
broke into fits of laughter.

"Stop it!" Hayri cried. "What's the matter with you? Laughing like a strumpet in front of all these people!"

And then there was another customer. He had a porter's pack strapped to his back and this gave him a stooping gait, but his shoulders were very broad. His face, hollow-cheeked, unshaven, with deep-set coal-black eyes, wore an expression of infinite sadness.

Gently, as though afraid to break it, he touched one of the cages.

"Say, lads, what have we here?"

"Birds," Hayri replied shortly.

"Dear me, what a lot of them!"

"That's right," Hayri said.

"And what are they for?"

"To fly," Hayri snapped.

Süleyman intervened hurriedly. "Of course they fly, but. . . Look, uncle, if you pay ten liras and buy one. . ."

"Then what?"

"You set it free and it'll take flight, up there." Süleyman pointed to the cloud. "It'll fly and wait for you at the gate of Paradise."

"Ah, so that's it. I see now," the porter said happily. "But ten lira's too much."

"We'll make if five for you," Hayri said.

Süleyman cast him an angry glance and tried again. But the porter drove a long hard bargain and in the end managed to obtain three birds for two and a half liras each. Then he went to sit on a bench under a tree beside the steps and, staring intently at the birds, kissed and caressed them gently, talking to them in a low voice all the time. It was impossible to make out what he was saying. Maybe he was speaking in another tongue and not Turkish at all. And suddenly a song

114

rose from under the tree, more like a moan, a long drawn-out lament. Like a flood of light, like a shimmering stream, pure and limpid, the song rippled softly under the noise and bustle of the square.

Süleyman's legs went weak and he sank onto the steps. The song had brought back everything, his mother, the kilim, Semih's betrayal, and he wanted to cry his heart out. Hayri, too, was touched to the quick. He felt himself stranded on a wide boundless stretch of sea. Mahmut went on smoking frenziedly, lighting one cigarette after another, gazing now at the porter, now at the boys and at the few stragglers who had stopped to listen to the singing. The whole of Taksim Square, the crowds, the motorcars and buses, and even the apartment buildings seemed to have fallen silent, holding their breath, giving ear to the song.

It broke off abruptly. The man stood up. Cradling the first bird delicately in his hand, he touched his lips to it and opened his palm. The little bird's head jerked to right and left, then with a quick flutter of its wings it darted up and away. A strange beauty, a brightness that was somehow very sad, suffused the porter's gaunt features. He looked after the vanishing bird, on tiptoe, as though he would take flight in its wake. In the same manner he released the other two birds he had bought and his arms fell to his sides.

"Go, little birds, go and carry greetings to my homeland," he murmured as he walked away, his back stooped once more. Without another look at Süleyman and the cages, he plunged into the tangle of traffic and crossed to the opposite pavement.

After this there was a small trickle of buyers. One old woman, wearing a shawl over her head, gave a cry of joy on catching sight of the birds.

"For my grandson!" she exclaimed. "I'd promised him, but it's three years now that I haven't come across a single bird seller. There aren't any left nowadays."

With trembling hands, she put a couple of birds carefully into a paper bag and hurried off into the crowd.

Such a human tide was surging through the square now that a pin could not have dropped down. People rushed about, shouting, howling, cars hooted their horns, the noise of engines, the clanking, the rattling. . . The odour of petrol, of burnt grease. . .

Süleyman's hopes rose. He waited and waited, but not a single person from all this crowd came forward to buy a bird.

He started shouting.

"Fly and be free! Hey, people, come up, come up! It's for 'fly and be free'. . ." His voice rose to breaking point. "For your Paradise! Paradise! To wait for you at the gates of Paradise. . . One bird, one Paradise. . . Fly these birds, free them. . ."

His neck craned towards the passers-by, he was yelling himself black in the face, but no one even turned to give him a look.

And then, as though he had suddenly gone mad, he started stamping on the steps, gesturing wildly and hurling the coarsest oaths at all and sundry. One or two people stopped and stared at this boy, thrashing on the steps, calling out insults and curses, then went their way. This made Süleyman redouble his swearing.

At one point, a lad wearing tight blue jeans and mud-caked shoes halted in front of Süleyman and admonished him.

116

"What's the idea, cursing everyone like this, you little bastard?" he growled. "No one wants your birds, that's all! Are people obliged to buy those birds just because you've caught them? Shut your trap, or else..."

His fists clenched, ready to strike; he was lunging at Süleyman when Hayri shot out like an arrow from where he had been crouching.

"Move off, will you, and double-quick too, if you want to live," he hissed. "We've got nothing to lose anyway..."

The youth had not bargained for this. Hayri evidently meant business. Spitting onto the steps, he hurried away, his fat buttocks rolling in the too-tight jeans.

Süleyman stopped cursing and hurled a gobbet of phlegm after the youth. Hayri did the same.

Feeling better now, Süleyman began to shout again.

"You see these birds?" he cried in ringing tones. "If you don't buy them and set them free, we're going to eat them all tonight."

He picked up one of the cages and, stepping down into the square, he waved it in the faces of the passers-by.

"Buy them, buy these birds and save their lives. Think, tonight we'll have to wring their necks and eat them... All of them..."

He smacked his lips.

"We will eat them. Yummy, fat juicy birds..."

Hayri also picked up a cage, planted himself on the steps and joined Süleyman.

"We will eat them. We will eat all of these poor birds..."

Mahmut sprang to his feet and grabbed a third cage.

"Look, people," he shouted. "See these hungry boys? They have nothing to eat but these little birds. If you don't buy them. . ."

"Why should they eat them?" someone asked.

"Because they need to. They're hungry. . ."

"They ought to do some useful work instead of wasting their time catching birds."

"Now, what kind of work is there that these kids could do?"

"Let them sell cigarettes."

Süleyman was still shouting, but his eyes were now on that meatball cart painted with flowers, on the smoking stovepipe.

All three of them went on shouting for a while, inventing all kinds of reasons for people to buy their birds.

Evening came, the sun set and the city lights went on. Yellow, red, green, orange, the neon signs of banks, stores, hotels, business companies began to blink and glow, and a haze of coloured light enveloped the city.

Exhausted, his voice quite hoarse now, Süleyman sank down upon the steps. Hayri came to sit beside him. Mahmut could not bring himself to look at them. So much trouble and pain, all for nothing. . . In the name of all humanity, of this milling crowd in Taksim Square, he was overcome with shame in front of the two boys, with pity for the doomed birds. Without a word, he turned away and slipped into the crowd.

The children were left there, alone on the steps. They looked very small now, both of them. Süleyman was leaning on one of the cages. His neck hung limply to one side. Hayri's head had sunk between his shoulders, so low it seemed stuck to his breast. The birds were silent now in their cages, too tired to flutter or even chirp any more.

Taksim Square was full to overflowing with evening crowds. From the posh hotel across the square the light of the huge neon sign fell over the cages, the boys, the steps, tainting them all a garish green.

14
~~~

"I'm going fishing," Mahmut said to me. "Right away, this evening. I may be going as far as Çanakkale."

He wore the dejected expression of a child whose toy has been broken.

"Good luck, good fishing," I wished him.

"Luck!" Mahmut gave a bitter laugh. "Luck indeed! Damn my luck!"

It was days since I had passed near the tent under the poplar tree. Once or twice I came across Tuğrul, and each time he shot me a pregnant look as though gloating over some bad news that he was not telling, laughing maliciously up his sleeve, like the low shameless son-of-a-bitch he was... No one had ever irritated me as much as this boy. I had always found him disagreeable. But now... I longed to give him a good spanking, the bastard, with his smug well-fed look. Because of him, because of those perfidious snake-in-the-grass eyes, I avoided going to the boys' tent. Because I knew there was something wrong there. Because only if some serious misfortune had befallen the boys could that odious Tuğrul have strutted about with such a self-satisfied air. Why else would a wretch like him, who had surely never had a taste of pure joy, why else would he suddenly be so pleased?

I tried to go to the tent. I wanted so much to see the

children, to find out what was up, but my feet always dragged me back.

One morning, I saw that red-winged bird of prey high up in the sky. The boys must be there still, I thought. They must have spotted the bird too. It'll buck them up. Now, I thought, now's the time to go down to Florya Plain. I only had to take the path that wound round the seaward side of the Air Force officers' houses and I would be able to see the tent and the poplar tree...

Instead, I went right down to Menekşe then up the slope again. The tall poplar tree seemed higher, larger than ever, its branches spreading far and wide, but there was no sign of the tent. I hurried up to where it had been and came upon Tuğrul crouching in his old place, his chin on his knees. He gazed at me with mocking triumphant eyes.

The place was covered with the coloured feathers of birds. They were everywhere, stuck to the copper branches of the thistles, fluttering in the breeze, mauve, red, green, white, blue, on the grass, the earth, the shrubs, the trees...

The hearth which the boys had built in front of the tent was black, with a few half-burnt sticks of wood smothered in a soilure of dead ashes between the three bricks. Nearby lay a large charred log.

I turned to Tuğrul and looked hard at him in anger and revulsion. But it meant nothing to him, at all. With that odious insolent smile on his face he fixed his eyes on the clump of dried thistles a little way off from the hearth. I took a few steps and stopped short, aghast, as I realised what he was looking at. My heart twinged with pity. On the dried grass, near a tall blue thistle

121

whose stem was plastered with tiny white snails, there lay a heap of bird's heads, hundreds of heads, rising as tall as the thistles. Yellow ants swarmed over these heads with the open lacklustre eyes.

From far-off Istanbul came the rumble of the city. Up in the sky, the rufous bird of prey was riding the wind, its large wings spread wide. And before me there rose a memorial to the callousness and the decadence of Istanbul town, to the oblivion of its past, of all that was human, to the loss of many many things, a memorial made with the heads of hundreds of tiny birds.

Also available in Minerva Paperback

MICHEL TOURNIER

Gemini

Jean and Paul are identical twins. Outsiders, even their parents, cannot tell them apart, and call them Jean-Paul. The mysterious bond between them excludes all others: they speak their own language; they are one perfectly harmonious unit; they are, in all innocence, lovers.

For Paul, this unity is paradise, but as they grow up Jean rebels against it. He takes a mistress and deserts his brother, but Paul sets out to follow him in a pilgrimage that leads all around the world, through places that reflect their separation – the mirrored halls of Venice; the Zen gardens of Japan, the newly-divided city of Berlin.

The exquisite love of Jean and Paul is set against the ugliness and the pain of human existence. *Gemini* is a novel of extraordinary proportions, intricate images and profound thought, in which Michel Tournier tells his fascinating story with an irresistible humour.

'His mentation and invention and imagination are sheerly wonderful. No other writer, now that Nabokov is dead, displays his fastidiousness, visual acuity and sublime waywardness . . . contains some of the finest descriptive writing that I have ever come upon' Jonathan Meades, *Books and Bookmen*

'Astonishing; an El Dorado of ideas' *New Statesman*

'The most extraordinary piece of writing for years, a disposition on the nature of twinship that is serious and intense but also mesmerizing' Salman Rushdie

ANTONIO SKÁRMETA

Burning Patience

Mario Jimenez enlists the help of Latin America's greatest poet, Pablo Neuda, to win the woman of his dreams in the witty, bitter-sweet tale of adolescent love set against the sadness of Chile's recent history.

'Set against the political backdrop of Allende's election and the eventual military overthrow of his government, the novel is a simple testimony to the power of poetry in people's daily lives'
City Limits

'The novel is . . . about power – not just the power of words but the power of ordinary people to survive violence and oppression with courage, integrity and even hope: with "burning patience"'
Marxism Today

'A master storyteller with a committed political conscience'
Literary Review

NEIL BISSOONDATH

A Casual Brutality

'In Neil Bissoondath's fine new novel, the atmosphere of
paranoia and tension created by the death-throes of a short-lived
financial boom on the small Caribbean island of Casaquemada is
sustained throughout by a tone which is both passionate and
ironic . . .

'As the story of a Casaquemadan doctor, Ramsingh, returning
from Canada, progresses, his gradual induction into the reality
of living in an increasingly anarchic and unstable society is
conveyed in sharp jolts of incident.

'*A Casual Brutality* is very much a description of colonialism
gone wrong . . . The false economic boom on Casaquemada has
become like a cancer: the island is dying but a 'cure' would
almost certainly kill. It is this dilemma that Bissoondath writes
about with great sensitivity and realism' *Guardian*

'A marvellously assured performance' *Financial Times*

'The book builds to a shattering climax. Like Naipaul,
Bissoondath is excellent at atmosphere, at place, at detail' Hanif
Kureishi, *New Statesman*

'An absorbing and very readable novel written with intelligence,
conviction and wit . . . "Promise", the usual word for first
novels, would be an insult here; this important book is a
complete, mature achievement' Hilary Mantel, *Weekend
Telegraph*

'A disturbing, original voice' *Independent*

EDUARDO GALEANO

Faces and Masks

Vivid and inspired, *Faces and Masks* is a unique fictional account
of Latin America, of a New World in the making. Here are the
voices of Simón Bolívar and Benito Juarez, Abraham Lincoln
and Teddy Roosevelt, echoes of an Inca defeat at Cuzco and the
fall of Davey Crockett at El Alamo, piracy in the Sierra Nevada
and the pioneering gold prospectors of California. Here is a
pageant of cowboys and gauchos, Coca-Cola and blue jeans,
Buffalo Bill and Sitting Bull, soccer and the tango, rubber, tin,
gold, and all those who lusted for control of the raw materials
and the lives the New World had to offer. Eduardo Galeano's
spicy blend of fiction, character and political irony brings to life
the Americas of the eighteenth and nineteenth centuries with
breathtaking imaginative power.

    Faces and Masks is the second volume in Eduardo Galeano's
trilogy, *Memory of Fire*, and continues the epic and moving
history of the Americas that was begun in *Genesis*.

'Galeano is an exceptional literary artist. He writes with the
intellectual translucency of Octavio Paz, the emotional clarity of
the early Carlos Fuentes and the sweeping visual acuity of Diego
Rivera . . . this reviewer awaits the third volume of *Memory of
Fire* with rapt anticipation' *San Francisco Examiner*

'An epic work of literary creation' *Washington Post*

A Selected List of Titles Available in Minerva

While every effort is made to keep prices low, it is sometimes necessary to increase prices at short notice. Mandarin Paperbacks reserves the right to show new retail prices on covers which may differ from those previously advertised in the text or elsewhere.

The prices shown below were correct at the time of going to press.

Fiction

☐	7493 9035 2	**Sassafras, Cypress and Indigo**	Ntozake Shange	£3.99 BX
☐	7493 9006 9	**The Tidewater Tales**	John Barth	£4.99 BX
☐	7493 9004 2	**A Casual Brutality**	Neil Bissoondath	£4.50 BX
☐	7493 9018 2	**Interior**	Justin Cartwright	£3.99 BC
☐	7493 9031 X	**The Bushwacked Piano**	Thomas McGuane	£4.50 BX
☐	7493 9000 X	**Faces and Masks**	Eduardo Galeano	£4.99 BX
☐	7493 9011 5	**Parable of the Blind**	Gert Hofmann	£3.99 BC
☐	7493 9010 7	**The Inventor**	Jakov Lind	£3.99 BC
☐	7493 9033 6	**Head of the Corner**	Grace Ingoldby	£3.99 BC

Non-Fiction

☐	7493 9012 3	**Days in the Life**	Jonathon Green	£4.99 BC
☐	7493 9019 0	**In Search of J D Salinger**	Ian Hamilton	£4.50 BX
☐	7493 9023 9	**Stealing from a Deep Place**	Brian Hall	£3.99 BX
☐	7493 9005 0	**The Orton Diaries**	John Lahr	£4.99 BC
☐	7493 9014 X	**Nora**	Brenda Maddox	£5.99 BC

All these books are available at your bookshop or newsagent, or can be ordered direct from the publisher. Just tick the titles you want and fill in the form below. Available in:
BX: British Commonwealth excluding Canada
BC: British Commonwealth including Canada

Mandarin Paperbacks, Cash Sales Department, PO Box 11, Falmouth, Cornwall TR10 9EN.

Please send cheque or postal order, no currency, for purchase price quoted and allow the following for postage and packing:

UK	55p for the first book, 22p for the second book and 14p for each additional book ordered to a maximum charge of £1.75.
BFPO and Eire	55p for the first book, 22p for the second book and 14p for each of the next seven books, thereafter 8p per book.
Overseas Customers	£1.00 for the first book plus 25p per copy for each additional book.

NAME (Block letters) ....

ADDRESS ....

....